PURSUED BY MAN-EATING BEASTS!

You are Omina, stepchild of the great Wizard Alcazar, and your efforts to rescue your step-father and free your land from the icy spell of Warzen, the Winter Wizard, have led you straight into danger.

Pursued by vicious, man-eating quagbeasts, you have taken refuge atop a snowy dune beside a clear pond. One of the huge-headed beasts is so close you can feel its foul breath hot on your skin! You must do something immediately!

1) You can dive into the pond and swim for your life. If this is your decision, turn to page 111.

2) You can blow your magic golden whistle, knowing it will help but not knowing how. If you choose to take a chance, turn to page 18.

3) Or you can choose to fight the quagbeast. If this is your decision, turn to page 147.

Whichever path you pick, you are sure to find adventure, as you seek to remove the
SPELL OF THE WINTER WIZARD

SPELL of the WINTER WIZARD

BY LINDA LOWERY

A DUNGEONS & DRAGONS™ ADVENTURE BOOK

Cover Art By Elmore
Interior Art by Jeffrey R. Busch

TSR, Inc.

To Christopher Bean
and his illimitable imaginings.

Distributed to the book trade in the United States by Random House Inc. and in Canada by Random House of Canada, Ltd.
Distributed in the United Kingdom by TSR (UK), Ltd.
Distributed to the toy and hobby trade by regional distributors.

DUNGEONS & DRAGONS, ENDLESS QUEST, and PICK A PATH TO ADVENTURE are trademarks owned by TSR, Inc.

D&D is a registered trademark owned by TSR, Inc.

First printing: August, 1983
Printed in the United States of America
Library of Congress Catalog Card Number: 83-50289
ISBN: 0-88038-054-3

9 8 7 6 5 4 3 2

TSR, Inc.
P.O. Box 756
Lake Geneva, WI 53147

TSR (UK), Ltd.
The Mill, Rathmore Road
Cambridge CB1 4AD
United Kingdom

You are about to set off on an adventure in which YOU will meet many dangers—and face many decisions. YOUR choices will determine how the story turns out. So be careful . . . you must choose wisely!

Do not read this book from beginning to end! Instead, as you are faced with a decision, follow the instructions and keep turning to the pages where your choices lead you until you come to an end. At any point, YOUR choice could bring success—or disaster!

You can read SPELL OF THE WINTER WIZARD many times, with many different results, so if you make an unwise choice, go back to the beginning and start again!

Good luck on YOUR adventure!

In this book, you are Omina, stepchild of Alcazar, the Wizard of Eternal Spring. You are out gathering herbs to use in soup for your ailing stepfather, when your peaceful evening is interrupted by warlike shouts and the thundering of many hooves. . . .

Stifling a scream of panic, you race across the fields toward home. The night is wild with the screeches of Warzen's boars. The cries echo through the countryside, and the thunder of hooves grows louder and louder.

"I should never have left Alcazar alone," you think, "not even while I picked the herbs for his soup."

You fling the handful of herbs on a bench and shout to your cat. "Hurry, Cornelius! We must get to Alcazar before Warzen's army reaches him!"

As you round the corner to the back of the cottage, your heart sinks. It's too late. Orcs are pounding on the front door.

You know you must hide quickly, so you burrow into the woodpile by the door, your eyes searching for the cat.

"Cornelius Silven!" you hiss, but he is gone. Suddenly you hear a loud BOOM!, followed by the sounds of the front door splintering, windows shattering, the army storming into the cottage.

"Poor Alcazar!" you think, but your thoughts freeze when you hear Warzen's voice bellow above the commotion.

"Silence!" he roars, and the noise stops instantly. "Well, well, well. Isn't this a sight to behold? The great Wizard of Eternal Spring lying in his bed, powerless before me."

The Winter Wizard's cruel laughter sends shivers up your spine. You crawl in deeper among the logs.

In your mind, you picture Warzen's ugly face—his black eyes glaring through narrow slits, his tangled beard packed thick with ice, his bared teeth as jagged as icicles.

"Where are your powers and your loyal followers now, Alcazar?" sneers Warzen. "I don't see anyone rushing forth to protect you."

"What should we do with him, Warzen?" asks a gruff voice. "Should we give him a few jabs with our pigstickers?"

Snorts and snuffles of rude laughter burst from the onlooking army.

"No, muttonhead," growls Warzen. "I want the pleasure of seeing him suffer. We'll put him in the Ice Cavern in my castle dungeon and watch him slowly freeze!"

"You hear that, Scrugg? The Ice Cavern!" gloats an orc.

"He can hang next to the disobedient boar with teeth as sharp as knife blades. It ought to be pretty hungry by now," howls another.

"Quiet!" booms Warzen. "Boarkeepers, get out your ropes and take him away! And see that you keep him alive on the journey north!"

There is a loud shuffling of feet, and you picture the horrible creatures tearing Alcazar from his bed and roughly binding his frail frame. It is all you can do to keep from leaping forth to defend him. Only Alcazar's earlier words of warning hold you back: "They are an army, and you are but one. If anything happens, you must protect yourself. You are dearer to me than my own life."

"And now the kingdom is ours!" shouts Warzen as the orcs cheer in triumph.

"Not for long," you vow silently. "Not for long!"

"Let the frigid winds blow! Let the wintry snows descend upon the land! Let all that is green and living turn to cold and darkness! The icy frost of winter shall reign forever!" booms Warzen, and the evil army thunders off, howling their victory cheer into the night.

A frigid wind roars across the woodpile, driving snow deep into the cracks of your hiding place. You shiver violently and begin to inch your way out from under the logs, listening for any boarkeepers Warzen may have left behind. Hearing nothing, you creep into the cottage and cover your trembling body with heavy blankets.

You try to rest, but your heart pounds madly and sleep won't come. There are many decisions to make before dawn. Somehow you must rescue your stepfather and restore him to health.

You recall what Alcazar told you earlier about the Crimson Flame Mushroom that grows in the Forbidden Forest. "It is the only cure for my illness," he said. "The Druids can help you to find it, but the forest teems with dangerous creatures, and you must be very careful."

Will you be able to find the Druids? Will they help you find the Crimson Flame Mushroom? Can you get it to Alcazar before it is too late?

Maybe you should try to rescue him first and search for the Druids later. But then again....

As dawn reveals the horizon, you have narrowed your choices down to two:

1) You can try to destroy Warzen first, then save Alcazar before he freezes. Turn to page 65.

2) You can seek out the Druids, find the Crimson Flame Mushroom, and take it to Alcazar. Turn to page 21.

Like lightning, you spin around on your heel and dash off, following the path back to Luna. From the darkness behind you a voice as rusty as an old horn screams.

"You are a fool! You've given up power and beauty! You'll never be happy now! You had your chance, and you've lost it!"

Not stopping to listen to any more of what the witch is shouting, you run, your heart beating in your temples.

"Omina!" cries Luna as you round the last turn by the fork in the road.

"Oh, Luna, you were right! There's a witch waiting on that path," you pant as you rush toward the tree limb where she is sitting. You stop short when you see her face. "Luna, you look awful! What's the matter?"

"It's so cold, Omina, and I'm afraid my wings are freezing. I can't move them at all anymore."

"Poor Luna!" you cry, taking her into your cupped hands and breathing lightly on her frozen wings.

"If I keep flying, the cold doesn't bother me, but as soon as I stay in one place too long, it creeps right into my veins." Her voice is fading to a whisper as her pale green wings droop.

"The frost is being melted by my breath now, Luna. Can you feel it?"

"Yes, it feels good."

"Here, I'll wrap you under my cloak to keep you warm," you say, placing the moth in your tunic pocket. "How's that? Do you feel better?"

"Much better, Omina. I should be all right soon."

"Thank goodness. Now, stay there. You can give me directions from there," you say. "I go down this path on the right, right?"

"That's right. Right to the right," peeps the little voice from your pocket.

Please turn to page 74.

You dig deep into your pocket and draw out your golden whistle. You keep it hidden in your hand as you raise it to your mouth, and then you take a deep breath and blow with all your might.

Music flows from the whistle and floats into the air. It is a soft, hypnotic tune, like a lullaby from a distant flute. You see the lilies grow drowsy, their heads drooping heavily onto their stems, their growling quieted.

Soon they fall into a deep slumber. The flute melody fades away, and the golden whistle disappears into thin air.

You grab your cloak and are pushing your way through the lily trunks, when suddenly you hear a nasty voice and angry words.

"Ouch! You kicked me, and I'm not the type that likes getting kicked around. Just watch where you're stepping!"

Down at your feet sits a clam, as big as your cat Cornelius, with a very annoyed look on its face. It has a sailor's cap perched on top of its head, and it's wearing a beautiful set of gold teeth.

"My goodness, I'm sorry," you say, panting from all the excitement. "I didn't even see you."

"Of course you didn't!" snaps the clam. "I'm just some insignificant little sea creature to you. I know that. But yesterday—yesterday you wouldn't have kicked me around, no, sir! Yesterday things were different."

"What do you mean, 'yesterday?'" you ask.

"Yesterday I was as tall as you are, maybe taller," snarls the clam, his teeth glittering in the sunlight. "I was the dockmaster down there on the shore, a human, just like you, running my boat on a fine hourly schedule to Etaknon."

"Etaknon? What's Etaknon?"

"The finest, most peaceful little island in these parts, that's all. A vacation wonderland. 'Come for a week, stay for a lifetime'—that's the motto of the Etaks, you see."

"So what happened to you? How did you get to be a clam?"

"How should I know? I went to bed at a reasonable hour, as always. You know, 'early to bed, early to rise.' That's my motto. And here I woke up a clam—and a clam in a snowstorm, no less! Thank goodness my gold teeth are still in place and my boat's here. That's all I can say."

You nod your head knowingly. "Now I get it," you say.

"Get what?" asks the clam impatiently. "Speak up. Get what?"

"It's Warzen's spell. He turned you into a clam so you couldn't get back to that lovely Enon Island."

"Etaknon," he corrects you. "Warzen? Warzen who? You mean the Wizard of Winter? Why that no-good, lousy, rotten excuse for a wizard," he growls, his gold teeth clacking loudly. "I'll get him for this . . . this . . . ." The clam stops, speechless.

"But how? That's the problem. He kidnapped my stepfather, too, and I've got to rescue him from Warzen right away. Any suggestions?"

"Let me think." The clam licks his teeth with a tongue that looks like a snake. "Sure, the Etaks can help us out. Their hearts are like gold—my favorite metal, in case you didn't notice."

"Well, how do we get there—to Etaknon, I mean—if you aren't running your hourly boats anymore?"

"Yes, that's a problem. Unless . . . ." The clam smiles a shiny smile. "Unless you can sail the boat over there."

"I'm not much of a sailor," you admit. "Especially in this weather." The wind is picking up now, blowing huge snowflakes into your face.

"That's okay," says the clam. "I'll navigate. But I can't do much more . . . without hands!"

"Well. . . ." You shoot a glance at the gold-painted wooden boat docked at the shoreline. Sailing isn't among your talents, but at least the boat looks all right.

"It looks pretty seaworthy from here," you say. "It would have a hard time getting through a snowstorm, though, wouldn't it?"

"My boat? My *Goldie?* She's the finest little vessel this side of the Balloon-Flower River. She's been through tempests, tornadoes, typhoons. A blizzard isn't going to stop her. She'll get us to Etaknon all right, like sailing on a dream."

You must decide if you want to travel with the clam or not. You have two choices:

1) Sail the boat with the clam to Etaknon. Turn to page 124.

2) Leave the clam and go on alone along the coast to Warzen's Castle. Turn to page 132.

You pull your whistle from your pocket. It gleams like a sunbeam in the snowy fog.

"Hurry!" shouts Cornelius. "Blow the whistle, Omina! The quagbeasts are nearly on top of us!"

With one shrill blast, you and the reindeer are whisked high into the air, bouncing like two kites in a March wind.

"Cornelius, we're flying!" you cry as the wind carries you toward the pool of water. Suddenly the whistle melts away in your hand, and you and the reindeer tumble into the icy waters below. The water is frigid, and you surface quickly and swim toward the nearest shore. As you haul yourself up onto the bank beside the snowy dune, Cornelius surfaces next to you.

"I'm not a bit wet!" he exclaims, shaking his fur.

"How strange . . . and look! What's that blue halo around your body?"

"I've no idea—but you have one, too." At the sound of a fierce grunt, Cornelius spins around. "Shhh! Don't budge!" he whispers.

Out of the corner of your eye, you see the herd of huge quagbeasts moving their heavy heads slowly from side to side, staring blankly from the snow mounds to the sky to the frozen fields.

You and Cornelius both have the same idea at once.

"They can't see us!" you both whisper.

You watch quietly as the bleary-eyed leader

turns and, letting out an unearthly bellow, lumbers back south across the tundra. The other beasts follow, grumbling to themselves.

"We're invisible!" you shout, jumping up and down and hugging Cornelius around the neck. "The water must be magic!"

"What luck!" says Cornelius. "But the spell is bound to wear off sooner or later. We'd better hurry on our way."

Please turn to page 54.

The moon is high in a pitch-black sky and you realize it must be midnight. Five hours till dawn. Five hours to hide silently, breathlessly, until the lilies close their petals and disappear for the day.

You settle down into the snow, quietly digging out a hollow to hide you from the monster plants. Protected between two big boulders, you wrap yourself in your cloak and roll up into a tight ball.

Your heart is beating so loudly you are afraid the lilies will hear, but you try to relax and think of good dreams to have, until you grow drowsy and finally drift off into slumber.

Suddenly you are jerked awake by sunlight streaming into your eyes, and you realize you have slept all night. You sit up stiffly, to discover that nothing has changed.

The monster lilies are standing, tall and ominous, all around, and now they see you. Their huge heads begin to dip in your direction, as if they have been waiting patiently for you all night.

Now you know you must take some action.

Please go back to page 144
and make another choice.

You pull on your warmest clothes: tall leather boots, two wool sweaters, and your heavy white cloak with the hood.

You know you will need weapons for the journey, so you pick up a sturdy iron poker from the hearth. "Let's see," you think. "I could use some magical protection as well. What can I take?"

Your stepfather kept a golden whistle for emergencies, hidden behind a loose stone in the fireplace. "The magic in the whistle will work just once, so use it wisely," he said. You take the magic whistle from its hiding place and drop it into your pocket.

Then, armed with the poker and the whistle, you head out toward the Forbidden Forest to find the Druids. Your heart sinks when you see that Warzen's spell has killed all the daffodils and tulips. The fields are deep in snow, and your legs are tired from trudging by the time you see the woods ahead.

The bare trees at the forest's edge cast long shadows across the snow, and even with the leaves gone, you see that these woods are thick and dark, with barely a snatch of gray sky showing through.

You were hoping for a sign or two: "DRUIDS TO THE RIGHT" or "INFORMATION SEVEN TREES AHEAD." But this is no civilized forest. All you see are tree trunks with deep, cold blackness lurking behind them. All you hear is the squeak of your own footsteps on the frozen, snowy ground.

.You are not even a mile into the woods when you hear mumbling, and you stop dead in your tracks to listen.

"Excellent peacock specimen," creaks a voice from the darkness. "My finest butterfly yet. Into the glass jar with you!"

You inch toward the sound, and soon you see a thatched roof held up by sawed-off tree trunks, all hung with icy mosquito netting. Inside sits a mousy little man in a safari hat, with a blanket thrown over his shoulders. He holds a blue-spotted butterfly in his hand. There is a wooden sign dangling over his desk: "PROFESSOR ERASMUS QUINCE, LEPIDOPTERIST."

"Excuse me, sir," you begin, pulling back the net door, now stiff with frost. "I wonder if you could tell me—"

"Just a moment. Just a moment." He drops the butterfly into a jar and clamps on the lid. "Did anyone ever tell you you're rather rude?" he asks, glaring at you through glasses so thick that they make his eyes look like blurry brown bugs.

"I was just—"

"Wait, wait! Hush up." He looks for a place to set down his jar, but the desk is cluttered with dusty books and maps and butterflies, so he shoves the jar into more clutter on a wooden shelf. Then he leans back on his stool and studies you from top to toe.

"An interesting specimen, I see. What are you? Elf? Halfling?"

"Human, sir. I'm human, just like you," you answer, a bit annoyed. "Can't you tell?"

"Quite. Quite," he says, wriggling his nose like a rat so his glasses jump up and down. He lifts up his hat and runs his fingers through his mouse-brown hair, making it stand straight up. "However, let's be specific. Let's be scientific about it. A child human, no doubt. A young Homo sapiens."

You can see now that he is wearing a vest covered with pockets, each with a different label: "PINS," "COTTON," "PENCILS." He reaches into the one labeled "MAGNIFYING GLASS" and motions for you to step forward.

"Open your mouth and let me see your teeth, child."

"Why would you want to do that?" you ask, shocked.

"To determine if you are correct, if you are indeed a Homo sapiens of a young age."

"Enough, sir. I don't have any time to waste," you protest. "I need to find the Druids, and I wonder if you could steer me in the right direction."

"Druids? Druids? No, I really can't help you. You see, I'm a lepidopterist, not an information center." He opens up a damp book and unsticks the pages, as if your conversation has come to an end.

You turn to go, but then your curiosity makes you stop.

"Professor Quince," you say, "what is a lepi—lepidopterist?"

"An entomologist specializing in the study of Lepidoptera," he rattles off. Then, raising his head to look at your stunned face, he adds, "A butterfly collector, child. Butterflies and moths. In fact, here comes one of my catches now."

A pale green moth with long tails on its wings flutters through the door and lights on the professor's desk, sending a delicate puff of dust into the air.

"Not much of a specimen, is she?" says the professor, wrinkling his rat nose at her. "Only one antenna. Not good enough to be pressed into one of my books."

The moth blushes a pale peach color and lowers her lashes over her golden eyes.

"But I suppose she's a decent guide," he adds. "She has a light in that one antenna, you see. Bizarre, isn't it?"

"That sounds very useful to me," you say, seeing that the professor is hurting the moth's feelings.

"Butterflies are not meant to be useful!" he barks. "They are meant to be beautiful. Without the beauty of their perfection, they are nothing!"

He slams the covers of the book together, ending the conversation. The moth darts off to a far corner, her wings trembling, and tries to hide behind a bottle.

"You've disturbed me enough for one day, child. Now be on your way."

"But wait, please. I have an idea . . . well, a

favor, really, to ask of you. I need a guide to get me through the forest, and I'm sure your moth could be of help. She could take me to the Druids, and then I'll send her right back. I promise you."

The moth peeks out from beneath her wing, her eyes glowing.

"What do you think, Luna?" the professor asks. "I'm busy with this peacock butterfly, and I would just as soon have you out of my hair for a while."

"Yes, yes! I'd love to be your guide," Luna says, all aflutter. "And I know a shortcut to the Druids' grove that will get you there in no time."

"She talks!" you exclaim.

"A strange and disappointing specimen, indeed. I told you," grumbles Professor Quince. "Well, go ahead and take her. But I need a deposit of five gold pieces to be sure you bring her back."

"But I don't have five gold pieces! I have no money with me!" you protest.

"Then you have no luna moth, either," he says, pulling the peacock butterfly from the jar and jabbing it with a pin. "And let me tell you this, young Homo sapiens—you will never make it through this forest without help. There are millions of creatures just waiting for a fine specimen like you. I guarantee that, if you go on alone, you will be dead by dawn."

You dig into your pockets, searching for something to use as a deposit. You have only one treasure, your magic whistle, which leaves you with two choices:

1) If you choose to leave your golden whistle as a deposit for Luna, turn to page 126.

2) If you choose to blow the whistle, hoping it will send you to the Druids, turn to page 28.

You rub your eyes, open them one at a time, and realize that you are somewhere very dark and very moist. There is moss growing on the walls. The only source of light is one doorway, a curved opening that leads outside, where the sun is shining.

"A tree trunk!" you say. "How in the world did I land inside a tree trunk?"

You shake your head, but it feels a little dizzy.

"That's funny. I can't remember . . ." you say, walking out into the sunlight.

You look up to see big cumulus clouds drifting across the sky, and you look down to see a little brown face peeking at you from behind a chinaberry tree. One by one, friendly halflings pop out from the trunk, smiling very big smiles and carrying fruit and flowers in their arms. Soon you are surrounded by a hundred of the tiny laughing creatures.

"Welcome to the Island of Etaknon, Omina," says one, handing you a bouquet of orchids.

"You know my name?" you ask.

"Of course we do. We are the Etaks."

"And we want you to be happy here," says another, giving you an enormous pink pear.

"How did I get here? Do you know that, too?" you ask the little creatures.

"The same way everyone gets here," answers one Etak with an armful of columbines. "Magic."

"We're here to make you happy," says another proudly.

"There's only one way to make me happy," you answer. "That's to help me find Warzen, the Winter Wizard, so I can rescue my stepfather."

"All in due time," say the Etaks in unison.

"We know of your problem," says the pear Etak, "and all problems have solutions, but you must be patient."

"But time is running out," you say, not the least bit patiently.

"Not to worry. Etaknon is not a place for worries," says a little creature, winding a yellow daisy into your hair. "Now come with us, Omina."

Please turn to page 62.

"Thank you for your kind offer," you say. You are suspicious of the elf's hospitality, suspicious of his tea and of his topaz ring. "We must travel all night to reach Krion's Castle by dawn."

"But the storm is fierce," warns Fiffergrund. "And besides, I was so looking forward to fixing a wonderful breakfast for you. Won't you reconsider?"

You glance longingly at the roaring fire, but then quickly turn to grab your cloak and reach for the doorknob. "No, thank you. We must be off."

A blast of icy air nearly topples you over as you start out into the howling storm.

"Good-bye," you shout over your shoulder.

"Please stop by and visit again anytime," you hear the elf call. Then the wind slams the door shut, and he is gone.

"Do you know the way, Cornelius? I can barely see anything!" you cry, your hands half-covering your eyes to shield them from the driving snow.

A fierce gust of wind screeches down from the sky and forms a funnel around the two of you, lifting you up and hurling you high into the snowy sky. Long, icy fingers whirl you around and around.

"Cornelius, I think we're in a tornado!" you scream, grabbing the hem of your cloak, which is flapping wildly above your head.

"It's no tornado, foolish child!" The wicked, laughing voice comes from deep within the funnel. "It's much more exciting than that. You see, I've been looking for you and that ridiculous antlered cat of yours, and now I've finally found you!"

"Warzen!" you scream.

"How clever of you to recognize me!" The evil voice taunts you as you are tossed higher and higher into the air. "And are you clever enough to know what I intend to do with you and your animal friend? Tell me, brilliant child, tell me!"

"Let me go!" you cry, your voice sounding very small amid the screeching of the wind.

"Never!" snarls Warzen. "You are finished now, and you shall never rescue your poor, sick wizard. No, clever child, you, too, shall suffer his fate—freezing to death!"

His evil voice rings in your head as pellets of hail lash your eyes and cheeks, and frost creeps into the depths of your heart. The wind whips you, tosses you, flings you high into the stormy clouds, drops you back into the icy fingers. You are helpless against this evil power.

Suddenly you and Cornelius are dashed to the ground with terrible force, your bodies shivering uncontrollably. Hard and cruel laughter fills the sky as the wind retreats into the storm. Warzen's voice trails off into the night, hissing, "Freeze . . . you shall freeze!"

"I'm finished, Omina," the reindeer whimpers, his chest heaving up and down.

"Cornelius, don't say that. We must always

have hope." But, inside, you feel far from hopeful. The cold white flakes are piling up all around you, and you know the winter night is long and dark. You wish it were spring, you wish you had your golden whistle, and you wish this were not . . .

THE END

"Let's just go right to Alcazar," you say. "There's no time to waste."

"No sooner said than done!" announces the alchemist, pulling a tiny vial of dark blue fluid from his sleeve. "Drink up, my pigeon. We'll be with your stepfather in no time!"

You take a gulp of the liquid, and CRASH! There is a flash of pink light all around, and there you are, lying flat on your back in the snow. From the corner of your eye you see jagged rocks and icy boulders all about, and waves pounding in from the sea just inches from your feet.

"Why, that darned alchemist!" you cry, sitting up to brush the snow from your cloak. "He didn't have a clue as to what he was doing! Save Alcazar, indeed! And where's Cornelius?"

One good scan of the seacoast tells you the reindeer is nowhere to be seen. But there is something else. Far, far to the north you see an enormous black castle perched high on a steep cliff.

"Warzen's Castle!" you shout, and as you scramble to your feet, you hear moaning from the cliffs behind you.

"Warzen's Castle!" echoes a hollow voice.

You spin around, searching the cliffs for a sign of life. But there is nothing, nothing at all.

"I'm hearing voices," you say, shaking your head. "What a terrific jolt I must have had landing here!"

"Warzen's Castle!" Again comes the voice from the cliffs. "Are you going to Warzen's Castle?" Now you can see a light, a lantern, deep inside a cave hidden in the bluffs. You squint to try to make out more, but only the lantern is visible.

"Who goes there?" you demand, trying to keep panic from rushing through your veins. "Who are you?"

"A very old boarkeeper," the hollow voice replies. "A boarkeeper who hung in the Ice Cavern at Warzen's Castle for many months."

"But I can't see you," you say. "Why can't I see you?"

"Because death saved me from my pain. Now my spirit wanders this lonely coast."

"A ghost!" you murmur, reaching to the ground for your iron poker. The lantern is moving slowly toward you now, out of the cave and across the rocks, and you feel your body begin to tremble.

"What do you want?" you shout.

"You are going to Warzen's Castle, aren't you?"

"Well . . . yes," you say, hesitating.

"I want to go with you," says the ghost, swinging its lantern as it approaches you. "I want to destroy the Winter Wizard. I want revenge."

"But how can we destroy him?" you ask.

"I have a method I've been planning for a century," the ghost answers. "I will tell you as we travel to the castle."

"But I can't even see you," you say.

"You want to see me? Then I will soon make myself visible to you. You will see every detail of my tortured form, the gashes from the iron chains that held my arms, the patches of frostbite that destroyed my body."

Your heart is in your throat now, and you back away from the voice ever so slowly.

"But I am on a mission of good—to save my stepfather—not on a wizard hunt," you tell the ghost.

"I don't care. I want revenge," wails the voice. "Revenge!"

The lantern is moving closer to you, over the rocks, across the snow. You must do something right away. You have three choices:

1) Ask the ghost to join you on the journey. Turn to place 118.

2) Run from the ghost. Turn to page 142.

3) Blow your golden whistle. Turn to page 28.

"This is a dangerous mission, and I mustn't involve anyone else in it," you say. "I'm going on alone."

"But, Omina, you need me. I can travel rapidly through snow and survive in this treacherous cold."

"I'm sorry. I've made my decision. I'm going on alone."

As you turn to leave, you look into the reindeer's soft, green eyes. They are so like Cornelius's that for a fleeting moment you wonder if you have made a mistake. But you harden your heart and turn away.

You have barely gone a hundred yards when you hear footsteps behind you. Before you turn to look back, you dig into your pocket and clasp your golden whistle tightly in your hand.

"If I'm in any danger," you say to yourself, "I'll blow the whistle and escape."

Just then a voice from behind you cries, "Omina, you must take me with you! I can't let you go alone!" It is the reindeer.

Before you can change your mind, you raise the whistle to your lips and blow with all your might.

Please turn to page 28.

Using Luna's light to help you see, you have your ropes untied within minutes.

"I'm glad those orcs tie such sloppy knots," you say gleefully, rubbing your sore wrists and ankles.

You sneak to the back of Erasmus Quince's hut and crawl beneath the mosquito netting, keeping low. The orcs are howling with glee, smashing the shelves with their pigstickers. Glass and butterflies and pins fly through the air and crash on the floor.

"Stop this minute, you fiends!" yells the professor as he scurries about the hut. He picks up wings and books, clutching them possessively, his nose wriggling like an angry rat's. "I have nothing of any value to you! Nothing at all! Get out of here and leave my things alone!"

"He's right, Thaug," growls Gorff. "This is all dead insects, dumb books, useless junk. We're wasting our time here. C'mon. I think we should get back to the castle before it gets any darker."

The orcs mope out the door, tired of their escapade. They hit a few more jars on the way, sending them to the floor with a crash. Erasmus Quince runs his fingers through his mousy hair again and again, shaking his head.

While all their backs are turned, you creep to the desk and open the drawer that holds the golden whistle.

"There it is, Luna," you whisper. "We're

safe now." Just as you reach for the whistle, the orcs charge back into the hut, yelling and waving their pigstickers.

"Where's the child, old man?" demands Thaug, grabbing the professor's vest in his fist.

"Tell us," threatens another orc, "or you'll end up pinned in a book like one of your precious butterflies!"

"Leave him alone!" cries Luna. "He doesn't even know we're here!"

"Hush, Luna!" you whisper furiously. But the orcs are already diving over the desk at you. Just before they grab you, you clutch the whistle in your hand and blow it, long and hard.

Suddenly you and Luna are surrounded by a golden cloud that whisks you right out the door and over the treetops. In a few moments, the cloud floats down and deposits you gently on the forest floor. You open your hand to see that your whistle has turned to gold dust in your palm.

"Luna, where are we?" you ask.

"I think we're very close to the Druid's Grove," she answers, shining her light in a circle around her. "Let me see now. We should go through this brush and pick up the path to the right."

Suddenly the moth shivers. "Brrrr! That trip over the treetops was very cold. I think my wings are frosting up."

"Here," you say, picking her up in both

hands. "I'm going to put you in my pocket, Luna, where it's nice and warm. You can give me directions from there."

"Okay," agrees Luna as you slide her gently into your tunic. "If you feel you're getting lost, just holler."

Please turn to page 74.

"It's very kind of you to offer to help, but we really must be on our way," you tell the alchemist.

"You mean that I stood here freezing all this time, and now you don't even wish my services? You are making a serious mistake, my little sparrow. There is no better alchemist in all of Urk—or anywhere else in the universe, for that matter. Allow me to ask again: may I be of service to you and your companion?"

"No, thank you, Mr. Ar . . . Fred, sir. My mind is made up."

"Well, my little dove, should you ever reconsider, feel free to contact me anytime. Here is my calling card."

As he hands you a sage leaf imprinted in gold powder, there is a sudden POOF!—and Glutias T. Argonimas disappears in a cloud of pink smoke.

"I'm glad he's gone, Cornelius," you say.

With hands clutching the reindeer's thick fur, you spring onto his back. Immediately he stretches out his powerful body and bounds off across the frozen fields.

With the wind whipping sleet into your eyes, you let your mind wander back to memories of sunny daffodils that once covered this barren land. It makes you feel very lonely, and you snuggle gratefully into Cornelius's fur, glad to have a friend.

Suddenly the reindeer pulls up short and whispers, "Listen, Omina! What is that sound?"

"It sounds like thunder."

"Almost, but not quite. I think it might be voices."

Now you hear it clearly. It is the howling of angry animals, and you turn to see an army of huge-headed beasts stampeding across the plain, their hoary breath making a great cloud in the frosty air. They are heading straight for you, foam dripping from their mouths, their eyes bloodred and glowing with rage.

"Quagbeasts!" you shout. "The quagbeasts from Willowup Swamp. They must have been driven mad by the cold!"

You cling tightly to Cornelius's neck as he races toward the Snow Dunes, the quagbeasts gaining at every step. The air, like icy fire, burns your lungs as you speed into the wind.

The dunes are slick with ice. Suddenly Cornelius's hooves slip out from under him, and he tumbles backward. You leap off his back to lessen the load.

The leader of the pack is almost upon you now, its foul breath hot on your skin. It lets out a wild growl and lunges at you. Before it can sink its teeth into you, you swing your poker as hard as you can, smashing it into the quagbeast's face. Blood spurts from a deep gash above its eye.

It lets out a loud howl of pain and shakes its head to clear the blood from its eye. You scramble up the icy hill on all fours and turn back to check on Cornelius. The quagbeast

bellows with rage, its one uninjured eye fixed on the reindeer.

"Cornelius, hurry!" you scream. "It's after you!" Digging in with his hooves, Cornelius clambers up the side of the icy dune and stops beside you, his eyes wide with horror.

After one futile attempt to scale the dune, the quagbeast leader pauses to consider its next move.

"Omina, look!" Cornelius cries.

Directly below you, on the far side of the dune, is a pond of clear water, sparkling like a star.

"Why hasn't it frozen?" you wonder aloud.

Then all thoughts cease as you hear the snarling of the beasts behind you. The leader has found a gentler slope and is lumbering up the dune, billows of cold steam pouring from its mouth, its red eyes hungry for warm flesh.

You must do something immediately. You decide you have three choices:

1) You can dive into the pond and swim for your life. Turn to page 111.

2) You can blow your golden whistle. Turn to page 18.

3) Or you can try to fight the quagbeasts. Turn to page 147.

"First I have to get these ropes loosened. Then we'll plan our attack. Here, Luna, shine your light on my hands."

You can hear the orcs slamming and crashing about the hut as you wriggle your hands free of the knots.

"That feels great," you say, rubbing the welts on your wrists. "Now give me some light down by my feet."

As you get to work untying the ankle ropes, you hear an orc shout, "She's trying to escape, Thaug! Look! The child's trying to escape!"

"Oh, she is, is she? Well, this time we'll get her once and for all. She's becoming a nuisance to us!"

"Get the butterfly nets!" a voice shouts.

You scramble to your feet as fast as you can. They are still tied together, and you hop off into the woods, with Luna guiding you. The orcs are chasing and gaining on you, thumping and squeaking across the snow.

Suddenly your rope catches on a tree root. CRASH! You land facedown on the forest floor. You struggle to stand, but before you can—WHOOSH!—a butterfly net surrounds your head, another entraps your feet and legs, and five orcs pile on top of you, tying the nets firmly in place.

"Help! Somebody help me!" you scream, trying to fight free of the netting.

In a flash, Erasmus Quince rushes out, whipping butterfly nets over the heads of the surprised orcs.

"You fiends!" he barks. "Let her go!" His rat nose is wriggling madly as he hops up and down in fury.

"Get the old man, Thaug!" you hear, and then, while you watch helplessly, the orcs close in on the professor. They wrap his body in netting and tie it tightly.

"Don't let the moth escape!" shouts Gorff, and in a moment, all three of you are trapped like Quince's specimens.

"Good work, men," snorts Thaug. "Now strap them onto the boars so they can have a bumpy ride back to the castle!"

The orcs snicker and cheer as they finish the job.

"We're going back across the fields so we won't get lost again. This way, men!" shouts Thaug.

"Off to Warzen!" yell the orcs, and the caravan bumps and snorts its way out of the forest and across the frozen fields of white.

Your head aches as it bounces up and down on the boar, and your heart sinks, for you can't see a way out this time. This time it looks like . . .

THE END

"Come, follow me," says the Druid priest. "I will prepare my unicorn for the journey."

Just as you turn to go, a terrible thought occurs to you.

"Luna," you say, clearing your throat to hide the sadness in your voice. "I just remembered something. I promised Professor Quince I'd send you back as soon as we found the mushroom. That means I'm on my own now. It's time for you to go."

"No, Omina, you can't do it. Please let me help you find Alcazar," she pleads. "There are many dangers still ahead, and I can always return to the professor later."

You can't bear to look at the little moth, for her golden eyes are filled with tears. You must make a choice:

1) Turn to page 121 if you wish to hold to the promise you made to Erasmus Quince and send Luna back.

2) Turn to page 151 if you wish to let Luna decide for herself and allow her to continue on your journey.

"Come on, Luna, let's make a run for it," you shout, heading back the way you came. There are trees blocking the path now, and you lift your iron poker high above your head and smash with it from one side to the other.

Now not just one tree is moaning, but the whole clump. Soon they are groaning in unison, and next, the crows on their branches are cawing, and now the forest sounds like a jungle of noises.

Suddenly a big, snowy branch bends down and raises you right off your feet, wrapping its needle-covered twigs around your body until you can't move. THUD! The iron poker drops to the forest floor, and now you are completely defenseless.

"Luna!" you cry, your eyes searching for your friend. "Where are you?"

"Over here, Omina," you hear Luna call. She has been captured by the branches of the tree next to you, and a nearby crow eyes her greedily.

"Scat!" You try to make a frightening sound, but the crow doesn't realize it. With a sigh of defeat, you can only watch the sky darken into night. Suddenly you hear wild screeches and snorts pierce the quiet of the forest.

"It's Warzen's army, Luna," you whisper. You are silent as the army approaches, and soon a handful of boars are sniffing and rooting at the trees, their boarkeepers shouting boisterously.

"There's the child!" yells an orc, pointing a

pigsticker toward you. "She's in that tree!"

"Get her down!" bellows another. "Just climb up there and whack off that branch she's hiding in!"

An eager orc scrambles up the tree. When he is high enough, he pulls out his sword and starts hacking at the limb. You begin to bounce up and down, and you hold on for dear life as you and the snowy branch tumble to the ground. As you jump to your feet, an orc knocks you down again, sits on you, and ties your hands and feet.

Blood drips down the trunk of the injured tree, and it moans in pain. Soon all the pines are waving their branches like giant arms, smashing orcs to the ground.

"Cut off their limbs!" shouts an orc boarkeeper, swinging his sword at an attacking tree. The pine raises a huge branch and knocks him to the earth.

Another orc shouts to a third, "He's out cold, Thaug! Scrugg's out cold!"

Now the orcs are chopping frantically, and the trees are moaning and swinging their limbs like enraged giants. You watch as orcs and boars and branches tumble left and right onto the snowy ground.

In all the commotion, it seems you are forgotten, and you slowly wriggle out of your ropes. Luna flutters down to your shoulder while you watch the continuing battle. Orcs are lying on their backs among bloody branches, trees are swinging wildly, swords are flying, and you are wondering if escape might be possible.

You have two choices:

1) Run ahead down the path to the Druids. Turn to page 81.

2) Hide beneath some broken branches until the orcs are gone. Turn to page 145.

The snow is piled in huge drifts, and the wind howls and shrieks around you. White tornadoes of snow drive bits of ice, like piercing arrows, into your face. You feel your skin growing numb.

"We can't go on in this blizzard!" shouts Cornelius, the wind carrying his voice over his shoulder. "We must find shelter!"

But there is nowhere to hide. The reindeer struggles on through the howling storm, battling the fierce wind at every step. Suddenly, just as you have all but given up hope, you see the faint outline of a thatched roof through the swirling curtain of snow.

"Look! I think that's a house!" cries Cornelius, hurrying forward as best he can.

Soon the building is clearly visible, a snug brick cottage with smoke pouring from its chimney. You jump off the reindeer's back and pound on the wooden door. Instantly it opens, revealing a handsome gray elf in a red silk jacket. He is beardless, and his golden hair, combed back, is as neat as a pin.

"Hooray! Company!" he cries happily, his violet eyes dancing. "I love visitors! And most particularly I love invisible visitors. Please come in." He bows deeply and motions to you to come in.

You exchange a guarded glance with Cornelius, but you are weary and numb with cold, and there is a cheery fire burning on the hearth. You enter, but cautiously, fearing a trap of some kind.

"Tea? A cup of hot chocolate?" asks the elf as he removes your cloak and hangs it on a peg near the door.

"No, thank you," you answer politely, not willing to trust him quite yet.

"Please sit down." He busily fluffs up the quilted cushions in the chairs by the fireside. "No tea? Then I shall be forced to sip alone."

He pads across the floor in his woolly slippers and plops down into a soft chair.

"I am Fiffergrund," he announces. "I live here alone, and, unlike most elves of my species, I love to entertain visitors. My talents are many: I can see all things invisible, read secret thoughts, and whip up a tasty stew."

He pours a drop of honey into his cup and fidgets with a copper ring he is wearing. It is very big for his little gray finger, and it holds a huge yellow stone.

"You are traveling to visit the Wizard Krion," he states. "I think that's an excellent decision," he goes on, ignoring your astonished reaction.

"Do you think he will help us fight Warzen and his orcs?" you ask.

"Unquestionably. He is a good and powerful wizard. And a great friend of mine," he adds, crossing one gray leg over the other. "You may have heard of his army of silver pegasi. They helped Krion and me when we slew the infamous Invisible Dragon of Drooglach just a century ago."

As Fiffergrund talks, you glance about the

inside of his tiny cottage. There is a watercolor painting of the Kingdom of Eternal Spring over the hearth. His kitchen is spotless, with lots of gleaming copper pots. A thick white bear rug lies before the fireplace.

"I am delighted you find my home pleasant," says the elf, smiling. Once again you are startled that he has read your thoughts.

"The ring helps," he says. "It is topaz set in copper, a wonderful instrument for mind reading." He jumps to his feet and tightens the silk belt on his jacket. "Now, I insist you both stay here tonight and get some rest. The blizzard will end by morning, and you can get a fresh start."

You try to object, but he won't listen.

"It is settled. Believe me, you are no bother. In fact, I am thrilled to have you here. Come. Let me show you to your room."

You must decide now whether to trust this elf.

1) You can choose to trust him and stay overnight. Turn to page 102.

2) You can decide you don't trust him and head out into the blizzard, hoping to find shelter elsewhere. Turn to page 31.

You clutch your iron poker tightly in both hands and slash at the thick stems of the lilies. They are as strong as tree trunks, but you chop with all your might. One weakens, oozing sap, and you hit it again until it collapses on a jagged rock.

Your arms feel shaky, rubbery. How can you fell the hundreds of flowers still standing, tall and strong, all around you? You take a deep breath and whip the poker above your head, slashing madly from one side to the other, running and stumbling, desperately trying to escape.

Suddenly you are lifted off the ground, and your head is surrounded by smooth, cool whiteness. You are being sucked into the center of a lily blossom! Your head is filled with a sweet, heavy fragrance that makes you sick and dizzy.

Your hand goes limp, letting the poker drop to the earth, and your body is drawn into the perfumed mouth of the lily. You feel yourself being swallowed whole, down into the thick, green stem. You are melting into the sweet odor, melting and blending, your skin turning as soft and green as the leaves and stem of the plant.

You have no fight left in you. Soon the savage plant will be satisfied. And for you it is ...

THE END

"Luna, can you talk to these trees?"

"I don't know their language, but I'll try," she says, lighting on a snowy branch of the bleeding tree. She flashes her little torch on and off. "We're sorry we hurt you," she begins.

There is no reaction. The earth rumbles beneath the roots of the firs as they keep moving toward you, slowly, menacingly.

"We didn't mean to harm you. We were just trying to get through." At this, the wounded tree lets out a long, angry groan that sends Luna flying off its branch and straight to your shoulder.

"There's just one other chance, Omina," she says. "Why don't you put some snow on the wound? Sometimes cold will take the pain away."

Luna flutters down and lights up the injury while you carefully press a handful of snow against the tree.

"I'm so sorry," you say. "I had no idea you would bleed. I never meant to hurt you."

You hear a deep sigh of relief from inside the tree trunk, and all the firs suddenly stand very still.

"A little more snow, Omina," directs the moth, like a tiny doctor with wings.

The cold seems to comfort the tree, and soon the bleeding stops and the pines rumble back to their places in the forest, settling their roots in the snowy ground. The wounded tree lets out a long, hollow cry, and right before your eyes, all the firs bend their lower branches to the forest floor to make a path in front of you.

"Why, thank you!" you exclaim, hiding your poker under your cloak. "That's very nice of you." You head down the road of pine needles, Luna's little torch flickering in the darkness before you.

You have barely left the fir trees behind when you come to a fork in the path. Each of the roads is lined with thick, icy trees. Each winds off into the same mysterious kind of darkness.

"Which is the shortcut, Luna?"

The moth points her antenna to the left, hesitating a bit. "But I feel something unusual about that path, Omina. It's danger—I feel danger."

"What kind of danger, Luna?"

"To tell the truth, I'm not sure. Could be goblins; could be spiders—or it could just be a few birds looking for a moth to snack on!"

"So maybe it's dangerous for you but not for me?" you ask. Luna nods slowly. "How long will it take to get to the Druids by the other path?"

"All night and then some," says the moth.

"And the path to the left?"

"Just an hour or so—if you don't run into trouble, that is."

"If I hide you in my cloak, will you take the shortcut with me?" you ask.

"No, Omina. I'm too afraid. I'd rather wait here for you to return with the mushroom, and then we'll go off to find Alcazar together."

You must decide which path to take. You can either:

1) Go alone and take the shortcut to the left. Turn to page 90.

2) Play it safe and take the path to the right. Turn to page 74.

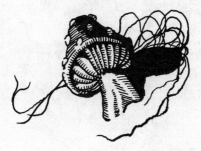

Two of the little Etaks grasp your hands, and soon you are being led into a straw hut, dim and peaceful inside, and full of the smell of rich earth.

"Here's where you'll stay," they all say at once. "We'll hang your name, Omina, on a sign above the doorway, and this will be your very own home."

Big pots of pink and fuchsia flowers hang from the rafters, and there is a tiny wooden bed, piled high with soft, pink pillows, in the corner.

"You even have your own desk, and beneath your bed, a handwoven carpet that creates beautiful dreams while you're sleeping." The Etaks giggle when your eyes open wide at the realization that the rug is made with real flowers and golden threads.

"But I didn't come to stay—" you begin, but you stop when the faces of the Etaks cloud over with disappointment. One little creature even begins to cry, a stricken look on its tiny face.

"But you must stay, at least for a night," says one.

"You will be so happy here, completely happy," says another.

"Well . . ." you say, looking at all the expectant faces as the halflings wait for your answer.

"Oh, please say yes," begs the littlest Etak, who is still crying tiny round tears as if its heart might burst.

They are waiting for your answer. You have only two choices:

1) Agree to stay, planning to spend just one night on Etaknon. Turn to page 149.

2) Tell them you cannot stay and get on with your business. Turn to page 69.

You throw your heavy white cloak over your tunic and fasten the hood. "I'll need plenty of protection," you think. You pull out a loose stone from the fireplace to reveal a secret hiding place. Inside is Alcazar's golden whistle, kept there for just such an emergency as this. You recall his words: "There is magic in this whistle, so use it wisely."

As you thrust the whistle deep into your pocket, you see the iron poker that rests on the hearth. "A good sturdy weapon," you think, and you pick it up.

Feeling safely armed, you hurry through the door, setting out for the evil wizard's castle. Warzen's winter spell has killed all the daffodils and tulips, turning the fields to frozen wasteland, and ahead of you lies a silent sea of snow.

Your first stop is the covered bridge, where you hope to find Cornelius Silven playing with the fish in the stream. It's always been his favorite hiding place. But now the stream is frozen, and you see strange footprints in the snow, as if a large animal has recently passed by. As you examine the prints, a gentle voice behind you says, "Those are mine, Omina."

You spin around—and find a large reindeer standing before you!

"How—how did you know my name?" you ask hesitantly, feeling bewildered. The furry, antlered creature looks friendly enough. His body is graceful, and thick lashes fringe his mild green eyes.

"Because I'm Cornelius Silven, your cat. Omina, something incredible has happened. Last night, while I slept here under the bridge, everything turned to winter, and when I woke up, I had become a reindeer. It's Warzen's spell, isn't it?"

You eye the animal suspiciously. You could be talking to Cornelius Silven, but then again, it could be one of Warzen's orcs trying to trick you.

"If you're really Cornelius Silven, then you can tell me all about Alcazar and his cottage, can't you?" you ask, crossing your arms over your chest. The reindeer nods.

"My cat always curled up next to the hearth. Tell me what the hearth is made of."

"Stones from the crocus fields," answers the reindeer without batting an eyelash.

"And what was I brewing last night in the kettle over the fire?"

"Herbal broth made with . . . uh . . . lemon balm and iris petals, I think."

You correct him. "Anise root. No iris."

"Now, Omina, be fair. I can't remember everything you put in your soups. And I truly am Cornelius Silven. Please trust me," the animal pleads, looking at you with Cornelius's forest green eyes. "And tell me what happened last night. Where's Alcazar?"

"All right, I'll tell you," you say, anxious to share the awful story with someone. "But I'm still not convinced you're my cat."

The reindeer listens intently as you relate

the details of Alcazar's capture and Warzen's spell.

"There is only one thing to do, Omina. We must get to Krion, the High Wizard of Yonbluth, right away. Since Alcazar helped him fight off Warzen's boars last year, he will surely help us."

"Krion!" you exclaim. "Of course! He's a great friend of Alcazar's, and he's just as powerful as Warzen."

"We must move swiftly, though, Omina. Come, jump on my back. We're going to pay a visit to Krion."

You must decide quickly whether to trust this unusual reindeer. It could be a trick of Warzen's to kidnap you, but it might also be the only way to save Alcazar.

1) Will you go with the reindeer to seek help from Krion? Turn to page 97.

2) Or will you decide not to trust the strange reindeer, but to go on alone across the tundra? Turn to page 38.

"I do appreciate your hospitality," you tell the Etaks, "but I am traveling on an important mission. I must save my stepfather from the Wizard Warzen right away. Alcazar is very ill, and he could die soon if I don't rescue him."

The halflings twitter among themselves like tiny tropical birds.

"Can you help me?" you plead.

"Unfortunately, we have no power," says the columbine Etak. "But ThorTak will certainly want to hear your story."

"ThorTak?" you ask.

"Our master," explains an Etak who is carrying a basket of red oranges.

"Come with us," say all the little halflings, taking your hands and leading you out the door.

"Where are we going?" you ask.

"To Mount Tak, where ThorTak lives," they say, and you follow them over green hills and down flowery valleys and up a very high mountain covered with fruit trees. The higher you travel, the foggier it gets. You realize you are walking through big, white cumulus clouds.

Soon you are standing on a mountain that feels like the top of the universe. It is thick with lush vegetation, and the trees are heavy with strange fruits.

"This way to ThorTak," announces an Etak, pointing to a path of flower petals that leads through the trees. "Just follow the path. It will lead to ThorTak. We will wait here for you."

You do as you are told, and soon you stand in a beautiful mountaintop clearing. In the middle of the clearing is a quiet blue lake. At the edge of the lake is a man, a massive, round-bellied man, who sits cooling his feet in the water. He is wearing a white deerskin tunic cinched at the waist with a vine. His long gray hair is entwined with a crown of bluebells.

"Well, don't just stand there," says the man in a jolly voice. "Come on in. Make yourself at home."

"Are you ThorTak?" you ask, looking him up and down. He has a hummingbird on his finger, but it flits away at the sound of your voice.

"That's what they say," he answers, laughing a friendly laugh. "ThorTak in the flesh." He extends a huge hand for you to shake. "And this is my house. I have the stars and clouds for my roof, the earth for my floor, and no walls to disturb the view. Now, what can I do for you, little one?"

"I have traveled from the Kingdom of Eternal Spring—" you begin.

"I know all that, Omina," he interrupts, waving his hand. "Just tell me what you need from me."

"I have come to you for help in fighting Warzen and rescuing Alcazar," you say, getting right to the point.

"The odds are great," he says, popping a

berry into his mouth. "Here, would you like one?" He passes a leaf filled with big purple berries toward you. You are hungry, so you take one.

"The odds, in fact," he continues, "are almost impossible for a little one like you. This Warzen is no weakling, you know."

"I know that, ThorTak. But I must try, in spite of all odds. I must save Alcazar."

ThorTak sets down his leaf of berries and looks you straight in the eye. "Now, tell me, my dear, how can a wizard be as important as all that?"

"Because he's my stepfather," you say, not batting an eyelash. "Because I love him."

"Precisely! Because you love him!" he shouts, leaping to his feet like a great elephant. "Yessir, that's the key to it all!

"Now, come here," he says, wrapping a burly arm around your shoulder like a polar bear. "I'll tell you something. I'm going to give you whatever you need to fight this Warzen devil. I'll see to it that his evil power is stopped, but the method we use will be up to you."

"You mean I have a choice?" you ask.

"Of course you have a choice. But I'll warn you right now: you must pay the consequences if you make the wrong decision. I believe in lessons, and we'll see how fast you learn, little one."

ThorTak leads you to the other side of the quiet lake.

"You see that castle over there?" he asks, pointing through the clouds toward the cliff on the mainland.

"That's Warzen's Castle," you say.

"Exactly," says ThorTak. "Now, every hour, the Winter Wizard walks out on his rooftop to check on his army. The next time he takes his little stroll will be the last time."

Your heart leaps. You have come to the right place for help.

"You have a decision to make," ThorTak continues. "If you want to use a nice, peaceful method of attack, we'll do it. It will work, but it will be quiet and pleasant.

"On the other hand, if you want, we can destroy him with his own cruel tactics. There will be thunder and lightning and a violent end. What do you say?"

Your mind is filled with thoughts of the terrible kidnapping, of Warzen watching your stepfather freeze in the Ice Cavern. And yet, you have never seen Alcazar resort to violence. . . .

"What's your choice?" asks ThorTak.

You must decide if you want to see Warzen suffer or if you just want to conquer him quietly.

1) Will you choose the violent spell? Turn to page 85.

2) Or will you choose the peaceful spell? Turn to page 113.

It is a night and a day of travel down the dark winding path, through snowy pines and frozen oaks and tulip trees, before you come upon a clearing in the forest.

"What a wonderful guide you are, Luna!" you cry. "We've found the Druids."

Luna pops her head out of your tunic pocket and peeks around to hear the strange chanting and mumbling coming from the clearing. You see a circle of hooded figures, all gathered around a blazing fire, their brown robes flowing to the ground.

"I'm afraid to approach them, Luna," you whisper.

"But we must, Omina. I'm sure they'll understand the importance of your request."

As you creep toward the fire, the mumbling gradually trails off, and one by one, the faces, shadowed deep in brown hoods, turn to look at you. A tall, silent figure steps out from the Druid ring.

"State your mission," demands the figure in a low voice.

"I am Omina, stepchild of the Wizard of Eternal Spring," you answer. "I have come to ask your help in curing the wizard of his grave illness."

"Go on."

"Only the Crimson Flame Mushroom can make him well again, and we are asking for your assistance to help us find it."

The hooded figure nods slowly, then turns to one of those behind him. "Aspirant, continue with the ritual. I will return to the circle momentarily."

"Yes, master," he answers, bowing, and the chanting resumes. The priest raises his staff and motions for you to follow him.

He travels calmly, with long strides, winding through the forest like an animal who knows each tree and shrub it passes. You speed after him, taking two steps to his one, past bramble bushes and spiderwort and buttercups withered from snow, until soon you find you are standing before a grove of chinaberry trees whose purple flowers have frozen from the cold.

"The place of the Crimson Flame," says the priest. "Silence, please."

He lifts his staff high and, closing his eyes, mumbles some strange words. Suddenly his staff vibrates with a soft musical sound. He bends down and pulls a bright red mushroom, round and shiny, from the brush beneath the chinaberry trees.

"Thank you. Oh, thank you," you cry, wrapping the Crimson Flame in a handful of moss and slipping it into your tunic.

"I know you are in a great hurry to deliver the mushroom," says the Druid, from the depths of his hood. "And I can get you to your destination quickly. I have a unicorn who travels with the speed of lightning. She will take you directly to your desired place. We must return to the grove to harness her.

"However, if you wish to take a risk, I shall transport you instantly by way of this giant chinaberry tree. You will arrive inside a similar tree close to your destination. I cannot guarantee the exact location of the arrival tree. That is the risk."

Which choice do you prefer?

1) If you wish to return to the Druid's Grove and take the unicorn, turn to page 49.

2) If you wish to leave instantly by way of the magical tree, turn to page 122.

"Alcazar desperately needs a remedy," you say. "Can you really help him?"

"Indeed I can. Let us get down to business," says Fred, pulling many tiny bottles from his sleeve and lining them up on the snow. The bottles glow with exotic colors: crystals of magenta, leaves of indigo, azure and scarlet and chartreuse powders.

"Curses!" cries Fred, searching his sleeves in dismay. "Where's my book? You don't happen to have an extra copy of *The Compleat Alchemist,* do you? I seem to have misplaced mine."

"Could this be it?" you ask, picking up a tattered book from the snow.

"How did you get that, you little toad?" snaps the alchemist, snatching it from your hands. "Since when do commoners rate technical manuals?"

"It's your book, sir, not mine. And please don't call me a little toad. Now, may we please talk about the remedy? It's for Alcazar. He has been fevered and pale and confined to his bed for the past month, and he's lost his powers of wizardry."

"Hmmmm," Fred mutters thoughtfully as he removes his broken spectacles and begins cleaning them with a crystal solution. Suddenly one of the lenses dissolves into a pool in his hand. "Confound it! Why am I using disappearing solvent to clean my spectacles? I think this weather is freezing my brain! I just can't think clearly."

"Please, Mr. Arglut . . . Fred . . . please pay attention."

"Certainly. Of course," he says, squinting through the frames of his glasses. "This could be expensive. The remedy, I mean. Indeed, I haven't treated a sick wizard in at least two or three centuries."

He flips through some pages in his manual. "Aha! . . . Oho! . . . Ah, here we have it!"

And quick as a rabbit, the alchemist leaps to his feet and begins mixing violet with rose, scarlet with buttercup. His hands are a blur as he opens, pours, closes, mashes, mixes, and stirs, until at last he presents you with a solution in a tiny bottle. The liquid is the color of a bright sapphire, and it glitters like a thousand jewels.

"Why, it's beautiful!" you cry. "But will it work?"

"I cannot tell a lie," says Fred solemnly, removing his purple hat and holding it over his heart. "I have taken this potion directly from my book. Since I have never dealt with this particular problem before and can give you no guarantees, I'll charge you ten percent less than the usual fee."

"If you've never made it before, how do you know it will cure Alcazar?"

"There is only one way to prove to you that it works. Try it yourself."

"Myself? Right here?"

"Why not? Just a small taste. If it doesn't make you feel fit as a fiddle, we'll try another

one—for which I will charge you the full fee, of course."

You glance from the blue solution to Cornelius Silven and back, not certain whether you dare to drink this strange and beautiful concoction.

"It's up to you," says Cornelius.

Obviously you have two choices:

1) You can test the remedy. Turn to page 95.

2) You can thank the alchemist for his offer but refuse to test the remedy and be on your way. Turn to page 43.

"Let's get out of here, Luna," you whisper, and turning on your heel, you race through the trees, crushing broken branches beneath your feet.

"The child's escaping!" shouts an orc from behind, and before you know it, three boar-keepers are on top of you. They tie you up again, roughly, making the ropes so tight they hurt.

"Ouch!" you scream. "You're hurting me!"

"Isn't that a shame, Gorff?" mocks an orc. "The child's delicate little wrists are hurting!"

"You haven't felt what pain is yet," snorts another, dragging you back toward the battle.

You see that the pines are tiring now, their branches hanging low and limp, their moaning quieted. The leader tree lowers his limbs to the ground, and the others follow, making an escape path for the orcs.

"They've surrendered, Thaug," says one of the boarkeepers. There are only five orcs left, and a few boars.

"Get the child and let's get out of here," shouts Thaug, mounting his boar.

The other orcs follow, their boars rushing down the path.

"Hey, are we going the right way?" asks Gorff suddenly.

"I don't know," answers another. "Scrugg's gone now, knocked out cold. He'd know how to get back to the castle."

"Look at the moss growing on the trees," says Thaug. "That'll tell us which way we're going. Come here, moth. Shine your light on this tree."

Luna flits over to Thaug, a worried look in her eyes.

"Sure enough. We're going the wrong way. Those lousy pines sent us the wrong way!" he shouts. "Moss grows on the north side of trees, right?"

"No!" pipes Luna, her voice unusually strong. "Don't you know that in the Forbidden Forest the moss grows on the south side? It's always been that way."

"I never knew—" you begin, but you say no more, for you see Luna shoot you a warning look.

"But, of course," Luna adds, "you boar-keepers would know all that."

"She's right," says Thaug. "I think Scrugg told us that once."

"Whatever you say," says another orc, and off they plod, down the path.

You pass what seems to be familiar territory, until you come upon a screened-in hut supported by tree trunks.

Luna flits back by your ear, whispering, "See? It's Professor Quince's hut. Now we have a chance to escape."

"Come on, men," Thaug commands. "Let's see what's inside."

Two of the orcs charge into the hut, their pigstickers drawn.

"You are trespassing on private property!" you hear Erasmus Quince bark. "Now, out with you! This is my laboratory. Get out!"

"This old man thinks he can tell us what to do, Gorff," snarls Thaug.

"Well, I think we should show him a thing or two, don't you?"

"Out of here, you brutes!" cries the professor. "And put those sticks down!"

You hear the scrambling of feet, the breaking of glass, and then Erasmus Quince shouting, "My butterflies! You can't do this to my butterflies, you idiots! I'll pickle both of your heads in a jar if you don't stop this very minute!"

"You've got that wrong, old man," snorts Thaug. "It's your head that will be rolling in a minute!"

The orcs outside are eager now, rubbing their palms together, ready to see some good fighting. Luna begins to squirm on your shoulder.

"Omina, we have to help Professor Quince. We can't just let the orcs kill him."

"But he wouldn't come to your rescue in a pinch, Luna," you say. "I don't see why we should risk our lives."

"No matter how nasty he's been to me, Omina, his life is in danger and we must help him."

"Our lives come first, Luna. I think we should sneak into the hut and take the golden whistle from his drawer. Maybe it will get us out of here and to a safe place."

The orcs outside can't hold off any longer.

They rush in to join the battle, and you have to make a quick decision. You may:

1) Try to steal the golden whistle. Turn to page 39.

2) Come to Professor Quince's rescue Turn to page 47.

"He's made Alcazar suffer so much. I want to get back at him the same way," you say. "Let him go violently."

ThorTak's eyes cloud over and you can see he is not happy with your decision. He shakes his head slightly.

"I will abide by your wish, little one," he says.

He snaps his fingers, and his hummingbird buzzes over and lights on his hand. "Gather my Etaks," he commands, and the hummingbird flits off.

Within seconds, a hundred halflings surround ThorTak.

"We are going to save Alcazar," he tells his flock. "You will hear a great explosion, thunder far in the distance, and when all is quiet again, you will lead the Wizard of Spring from the Ice Cavern through the underground tunnel and straight to my house," he orders.

"Yes, ThorTak," say the Etaks in unison. "We will do it."

"There will be no danger for you," he tells them. "Now go." With that, all the little brown halflings disappear.

You stand next to ThorTak waiting for Warzen to walk out on his rooftop. The moment he appears, ThorTak sighs deeply and you can feel the energy building in his huge body. It is as though he is growing larger and larger right before your eyes.

Suddenly he extends his arm toward the rooftop, and magically, four fiery meteors of

red and yellow and green and blue spring from his fingers and shoot into the sky. They streak way across the water, leaving an arched path of dazzling colored sparks floating in the air behind them.

In an instant, the sparks reach the Winter Wizard and form a diamond around his body. Before Warzen can move to defend himself—BOOM! There is a terrible explosion. The meteors burst into blinding bright light, and colors fly in every direction. You hear a howl of anguish from the wizard, and you clasp your trembling hands hard against your ears to block out the cry.

When you open your eyes, the sparks have died away, and Warzen has disappeared from the face of the earth.

ThorTak sighs a long, tired sigh and turns toward you.

"There you are, little one. Warzen is gone, a victim of great and terrible violence. How do you feel?"

"A little shaken up," you say, "but happy that he's gone."

"My Etaks are bringing Alcazar here now," he says quietly. "He has been cured, and spring is already returning to your kingdom." ThorTak lays a big hand on your small shoulder. "Now, my little one, you have a lesson to learn."

Suddenly you are afraid. You feel very small next to this enormous, powerful being.

"We here on Etaknon have a commitment.

It is a commitment to peace. I used my power in a violent way because that was your request. But we had a peaceful alternative, and we only resort to violence when it is absolutely necessary."

"What are you going to do with me?" you ask.

"I am not going to hurt you. That is a promise. But you must learn the ways of peace while you are here. Alcazar will be returning home immediately. But you, my little one— you will stay here on Etaknon until you understand the meaning of peace and gentleness, until you understand that violence is not the best way to fight violence. The power of peace is a great one."

"But how long will that be?" you ask, on the brink of tears. "How long am I going to have to stay here?"

"As long as you make it. As long as it takes you to learn. Maybe a day, maybe a lifetime. It's up to you."

"But that means I may never see Alcazar again!" you cry.

"Perhaps. But between you and me, little one, I don't think it will take you long. I'd say you look like a pretty fast learner, wouldn't you?"

You nod. "Yes, at least I hope so. I want to learn quickly."

"And the lesson will last a lifetime," says ThorTak, taking your hands in his. "Now go to your hut. You know where it is. And the

Etaks will be there shortly to begin your lessons."

"Yes, ThorTak," you say, knowing that you must take responsibility for the decision you made. You follow the flower petal path down Mount Tak, through the fruit trees, and into the valley, toward your little hut by the sea.

THE END

"I'm going to try the shortcut, Luna," you announce. "I've got to take the chance. I want to get that mushroom before Alcazar freezes."

"I'll wait here as long as I can, Omina," says the moth, shivering. "But hurry—my wings are frosting over from the cold."

You make your way through the woods, the frozen leaves squeaking underfoot as you walk. The forest is damp and dark, and strange hootings and hissings tell you that you're not alone—unseen spirits lurk beyond your vision. You feel a presence behind you and jerk your head around to see—nothing. Nothing but trees and vines and . . . .

"Such a sweet puff of pastry," creaks a voice right in your ear. "And all alone in such a big forest."

You spin about, ready to draw your iron poker, and there stands an old woman with a face as wrinkled as a dried mushroom. She is wearing a veil and gown of black linen, and her eyes are yellow with age.

"I am Madame Wortroot. Would you care for one of my mushrooms?"

She hobbles over to a tree stump and slings her shoulder sack down. Big and little mushrooms spill out onto the frozen ground.

"This one," she croaks, pinching a soft orange one between her fingernails, "this one will give you wealth, great wealth. Just one bite, and you will be richer than a king."

You watch her silently, your hand on your iron poker.

"Aha! It's not riches you are after? Then power is what you want." She digs through her sack, then thrusts a lumpy green mushroom against your chest.

"Here, try this," she says. "It will give you all the power you ever wanted. You can get even with all your enemies, forcing them to their knees to beg your forgiveness." She lets out a cackle, her mouth wide open, and her teeth look like rotted toadstools.

"You're a witch, aren't you?" you ask boldly. "I've never seen a witch face-to-face before."

"Ah, you are very perceptive for a young thing," she says, pinching your cheek between her wrinkled fingers. You back away, not wanting her to touch you.

"Yes, I am a witch, but not your ordinary wicked breed of witch. I, my cream puff, am a good witch, the keeper of the three secrets to happiness—wealth, beauty, and power."

Your eyes narrow in disbelief.

"Oh, I know this old face can be deceiving, but I am telling the truth. My mushrooms carry great powers. Watch!" she insists, pointing her crooked finger to make a chair appear out of nowhere. "Now, sit down, my pudding. I have something magical and wonderful to show you."

She nibbles on a hairy red mushroom. "The key to beauty," she says, and soon she is twirling around, her aprons, skirts, and sleeves flying about in the air. Around and around she goes, faster and faster, until she disappears in a blur, just a spinning funnel of black fabric. WHOOSH! With a jolt, she stops, and in her place there stands a most extraordinary sight.

A slim woman with hair like sunbeams, eyes of sapphire, skin rich as cream stands before you.

"You see?" she purrs, her voice as smooth as silk. "My diamonds are from the Ardian Caves. My gold is mined in the depths of the Slove Mountains, and I wear perfume from Gressia. My beauty can buy me anything on earth."

"That means nothing," you say. "Beauty isn't the key to life, and neither are power and riches. Alcazar has always taught me—"

"I know what you intend to say," says Madame Wortroot as she arranges the bangles on her wrist. "That love and goodness are the secrets to happiness."

"Exactly!"

The witch shakes her blond head, smiling. "Poor Alcazar. Look what goodness got him—a free ticket to Warzen's Ice Cavern."

"How did you know that?" you demand.

"We good witches know many things. And I certainly know that you don't want to end up hanging next to your stepfather like a side of beef. Make Warzen your slave. Make him pay for his cruelty," she says, snatching up a lumpy green mushroom and sticking it under your nose.

"Eat this mushroom of power, sweet cream

puff, and the whole world will be at your feet."
You have two choices:

1) Take a bite, hoping it will give you
   power over Warzen. Turn to page 119.

2) Run from the witch and go back to find
   Luna. Turn to page 11.

"Well, I suppose I should test it rather than take a chance on hurting Alcazar with the wrong medicine." You uncap the bottle carefully, and you and Cornelius each place a tiny drop on your tongues.

"Ouch! It burns!" you shout, jumping up and down in the snow.

"No, no, no! According to the book, it doesn't burn!" says Fred quickly. "It says so right here on page eleven hundred: 'Very soothing to the palate.'"

"The book is wrong! It burns! And look," you shout, "it's turning my skin hard and brown!"

Suddenly everything around you seems to be growing taller.

"You're shrinking!" cries Cornelius.

"You're shrinking, too!" you shriek.

"And you're turning into . . . oh, my!" Fred's voice is trembling. "I have no remedy for this! I'm powerless. You're both turning into nasty little brown cockroaches!"

"Help me, you faker!" you scream, shaking your antennae furiously. "Do something! Change us back!"

"I'm terribly sorry, but I'm afraid there's nothing I can do. It's the cursed book, I tell you. They just don't keep these things up to date," he complains, hurriedly stuffing bottles into his sleeves. "Drat it, anyway! Please accept the most sincere apologies from Glutias T. Argonimas. And you can be certain I'll write a nasty letter to the publisher!"

With that, he vanishes in a puff of pink smoke.

"Drat YOURSELF!" you scream as you scurry off to find a safe hiding place, with Cornelius right behind.

As you squeeze under the protection of a nearby rock, you realize the utter hopelessness of the situation. It is clearly . . .

THE END

Hopping onto Cornelius's back, you wrap your arms around his soft neck, and your mount gallops northeast toward the Kingdom of Yonbluth. You bury your face deep in his fur to shield it from the bitter, stinging wind.

You have barely passed the Hill of Sweet William when—POOF!—a dead tree on your right disappears in a cloud of pink smoke. Cornelius skids to a halt.

"Ach! Ahem! Ugh!" A curious little man in a purple robe is coughing and waving his hands to clear away the smoke. His wide-brimmed hat is so much too big that it rides down over his eyes.

"Darned hat! I must speak to my haberdasher when I get back," he complains, pushing the hat back up on his forehead. "How many times do I have to tell him to trim the hats and beef up the robes? The lining in this robe is entirely too thin!" A huge shudder shakes the man's skinny little frame. "I'm FREEZING!"

Cornelius takes a few steps back, and you rub your eyes to see through the pink haze, which is now settling. The strange little man picks up a pair of broken spectacles from the snow and places them on his nose. "He looks just like a prune with weak eyes," you think.

"Curses!" he grumps. "Everywhere I go, I run into crowds. Can't an alchemist have a little peace and quiet? Who are you, anyway?"

"I . . . I am Omina," you tell him. "And this is my cat, Cornelius Silven."

"Cat? Cat, did you say?" The alchemist looks at you as if you are mad. "What manner of kingdom is this, where cats look like reindeer?" He shakes his head in disbelief.

"Well, actually, Cornelius WAS my cat," you try to explain, "but the Winter Wizard turned him into a reindeer just last night. And to answer your other question, you are now in the Kingdom of Eternal Spring."

"Spring?" he asks disgustedly. "Spring? Then why are my teeth chattering? This looks like the dead of winter to me!"

"That's because of the spell. You see, it's been spring here as long as I can remember, but my stepfather, who is also the Wizard Alcazar, fell ill and lost his power, and. . . ." You can see that the alchemist doesn't understand a single word, and you decide to stop before your story becomes even more jumbled and confusing.

"Never mind all that," you say. "Just tell us who YOU are. And how did you get here? And what was that pink smoke?"

"I, my young pigeon, am the one and only Glutias T. Argonimas, alchemist extraordinaire, adviser to young and old, tall and short." He removes his hat and makes a dramatic bow, exposing a bald head as shiny as a crystal ball. "How may I be of help?"

"Well, I don't really know, Mr. Arglut . . . Arglon. . . ."

He waves his hand irritably. "Just call me Fred. That will do."

"Well, Mr. Fred, what sorts of things do you do?"

"Anything. Everything. I cure the ill, sicken the well, fatten the thin, bring joy to the downhearted. I can make any kind of potion you need. I can solve all your problems. Er—you do have a problem, don't you?" he asks eagerly.

"As a matter of fact, I do. But how do you know you can solve it?"

"You insult me, little nightingale," he whimpers, clasping his wrinkled hands to his chest. "I am hurt—cut to the quick."

He reaches into his breast pocket and removes a yellowed sheet of paper, which he flashes before your eyes. "'School of Alchemy, Kingdom of Urk,'" he reads, then stuffs the paper back into his pocket. "Now, if you have need of my services, you must hurry. I am going to disappear shortly, before I catch my death of—ACHOOO!"

"Gesundheit!" says Cornelius, watching the alchemist noisily blow his nose into an enormous red handkerchief.

"Let me put it this way, Fred," you say, all business. "I need a cure for someone who is very sick but also very far away. What would you suggest?"

"Simplicity itself, little dove!" answers the alchemist, cramming his hanky under his hat. "I can—POOF!—concoct a potion that will survive a trip of any distance. Or we can all—POOF!—disappear, only to reappear in the patient's room, so I can have a look at him. But I've got to do either 'POOF!' quickly, before all my herbs freeze."

You examine the little man a moment, your mind racing. It appears that you have three choices:

1) You can ask the alchemist to make a potion for you and take it directly to Warzen's Castle. Turn to page 77.

2) You can have the alchemist make you disappear, then reappear with Cornelius in the Ice Cavern. Turn to page 35.

3) Or you can thank the alchemist for his offer but refuse his services. Turn to page 43.

The storm hurls hail as big as walnuts against the window, and the wind whips and screeches around Fiffergrund's chimney. You are dead tired, and you know that there is no way you can survive a night out in the vicious weather.

"Splendid!" exclaims Fiffergrund as he pulls two plump quilts from a cedar trunk. "I knew you'd decide to stay."

He makes up the straw bed for you with clean white sheets and arranges one quilt for Cornelius.

"Can I get you something else? A little warm milk? Some biscuits?"

"No, thank you," you answer, your eyes heavy with sleep. "This is quite enough."

"Good night," whispers the elf. "Sweet dreams to you both."

As he shuts the door, you hear Cornelius settle in the corner, and you float off into a restless slumber, your mind filled with dreams of elves and giants and murky, menacing shadows.

Next thing you know, sunlight is streaming through the lacy curtains.

"Cornelius, time to get up," you say, flipping back the bed linens. "We made it through the night, and it looks as if the blizzard is all over."

"What luck!" says the reindeer. "And smell that bread!"

You are up and into the kitchen in no time. There is Fiffergrund, a sturdy apron tied around his waist, dishing up two bowls of steaming porridge. On the table are baskets of dark and light breads, plates of herb butter and honey, and huge mounds of black and red berries.

"Good morning! I'm so pleased you slept well," says the elf, who has clearly been bustling about since dawn. "Look at you—it seems you are quite visible again this morning."

"He's right, Cornelius! Our blue halos are gone!" you exclaim, your mouth already full of raspberries.

You devour breakfast, while Cornelius nibbles on reindeer moss. "I scraped it off the rocks outside. It grows right under the snow," explains Fiffergrund, and then, nonstop, he chatters on. "Now, the shortest route to Krion's is along the river, where the balloon flowers used to grow. Here, I'll make you a quick map." He scribbles some arrows and lines on a parchment placemat, explaining every detail carefully.

The moment your food is on its way to your stomach, you push your chair back from the table.

"I don't mean to be rude," you say, "but we must be on our way. I'll just grab my cloak from the peg over here . . . ."

"Wait, wait!" cries the elf. He hops to his feet and chases after you. "Don't be in such a rush. Why not spend a few days here with me, to rest up? I'll feed you well so you'll have plenty of strength for the journey ahead. You'll need it."

"That's very kind of you, but we must hurry to free Alcazar," you say, pulling your hood up around your face. You shoot a quick glance at Cornelius, then turn back to the elf. "Perhaps you'd like to join us on our mission."

"Join you? What a splendid idea!" shouts Fiffergrund. "Here—I'll just throw some fruit and bread into a bag and put on my topaz ring, and we'll be ready in a wink."

"Are you sure about this?" Cornelius whispers in your ear.

"Of course!" pipes Fiffergrund from the kitchen, where he is hanging his apron on a little brass hook. "I can be trusted, believe me, and, besides, I'm not a bad fighter. Warzen will be sorry he ever got so greedy, let me tell you."

Off you go with the elf and the reindeer and your burlap bag full of food. You have not traveled far along the river when you see a sign stuck in the snow: "KINGDOM OF YONBLUTH."

Rising in the distance before you is a magnificent ice structure, topped with turrets and towers, its roof mounded high with snow. Icicles dangle from every gable, glistening like silver in the sunlight.

"Krion's Castle!" gasps Cornelius. "Isn't it amazing?"

"What is truly amazing is that Krion's Castle was never made of ice before, but of stone," says Fiffergrund, pursing his lips and rubbing his chin. "Something smells of Warzen here."

"Let's find out what's going on," you say. "Let's find Krion."

You and Cornelius rush toward the castle and plaster your ears against the door, listening for any sound. Suddenly—BOOM!—the door flies open, sending you both crashing to the snowy floor inside. Right in front of you are two huge feet, wrapped in leather and as big as boulders.

You slowly and carefully raise your head to see what is attached to those enormous feet. There, right before your eyes, stands a frost giant, as tall as an oak tree, his head a mane of wild golden hair, his blue eyes as cold as ice. He leans on his ice scepter and stares first at you, then at Cornelius.

"Um, excuse me, sir. My name is . . . ah . . . Omina," you stammer, rising to your feet. "I am the stepchild of Alcazar, Wizard of Eternal Spring."

"And I am Cornelius Silven, loyal cat of the wizard," says the reindeer.

The giant strokes his golden beard with his hand. "Cat?" he roars fiercely. Icicles shatter from the boom of his voice, thundering to the floor like alarum bells.

"Well, a cat until yesterday," explains Cornelius, his green eyes very wide and very frightened, "until. . . ."

"Until Warzen turned your kingdom to winter, and you to a reindeer?" bellows the frost giant. Icicles are now crashing to the ground by the hundreds, and you raise your arms above your head for protection from the frozen shower.

The giant steps across the room, shaking the walls of his castle with every step. "Is that it? Did Warzen turn you into a reindeer? Is that what happened?"

"Why, yes," you and Cornelius both say at once. "How did you know?"

"Because he is Krion!" shouts Fiffergrund, bouncing through the doorway. "And Warzen has turned him into a frost giant! Am I right, friend?" asks the elf, hopping with curiosity. "Am I right?"

"You are right, Fiffergrund, so right. And I have no power to change myself back. I am a wizard in my heart, and a big, dumb giant in my body," he moans, sitting down on a mound of ice, his huge head in his hands. "Do you know what that means?"

"Everyone is afraid of you now, aren't they?" you ask.

"Yes," he says, nodding sadly. "Friends won't visit because they are frightened, and I'm lonely, so lonely. What am I to do?"

Fiffergrund sighs and plops down on the giant's leather shoe. "Somehow we will find a way, Krion. Remember when they said the Invisible Dragon of Drooglach could never be slain? Everybody said so. But we destroyed it, didn't we?" the elf says encouragingly.

"What power do I have to conquer Warzen

and his army?" moans Krion. "I'm worthless, nothing but a big, clumsy giant."

"Not true!" you cry, before Fiffergrund can get a word in. "Think of how strong you are now. You could pick Warzen up in one hand if you had to, and throw him halfway across his kingdom."

"Yes, you're right. I do have strength," he admits.

"And what about your pegasi?" asks Fiffergrund. "Where are they? What happened to them? Warzen didn't turn them into groundhogs, did he?"

"No, as a matter of fact, he didn't," says Krion, his icy eyes coming alive.

"Now, the final question, the most important question—what about your magic powers?" asks Fiffergrund.

The giant's shoulders droop and his eyes cloud over. "I suppose they've disappeared. I've been afraid even to try a simple spell, because I can't bear to know the truth. I don't want to know if they're gone."

"Krion, I have a hunch that Warzen wasn't able to take all your powers away. I bet there's plenty of wizardry left someplace deep in that giant's body."

Krion runs his thick fingers through his golden hair.

"All right," he says. "I'll give it a try. Let me see if I can turn that icicle into a carrot. Once this would have been a simple matter, but now it makes my heart flutter like a bird's . . . ."

He shuts his eyes in concentration for a moment, and then—POOF! A beautiful orange carrot tumbles to the ground.

"You did it!" shouts the elf gleefully.

"Here, this is for you," says the wizard, handing the carrot to Cornelius. "And now, I'd say we've wasted enough time. I'm ready to demonstrate to Warzen just how powerless he truly is."

"Me, too!" says Cornelius.

"A cat to a reindeer, indeed!" huffs Krion, heading out the door with Cornelius by his side.

"A wizard to a giant, indeed!" blusters the reindeer.

Just as you start off behind them, Fiffergrund grasps your arm and pulls you aside. "Omina, I want you to think about something," he says. "You are very important to Alcazar, and he will want to know that you are safe. If you come with us, there are no guarantees that you will survive Warzen's wrath. Perhaps you should wait here and let us fight Warzen on our own."

"But that wouldn't be fair, would it?" you ask. "After all, this mission was my idea, and I should stick with it to the end, in spite of the danger."

"You want to be alive to see Alcazar again, don't you? The three of us are well equipped for battle, and I truly believe we can conquer Warzen if we keep our heads together."

The elf puts both hairy hands on your

shoulders. "Think about it. We'll be waiting outside for your decision."

With that, Fiffergrund disappears out the door. You want to be fair, but you also want to be alive to see Alcazar again. What will you do?

1) Will you let the others fight, knowing you are safe and sound in Yonbluth? Turn to page 131.

2) Will you risk your life and go into battle with the others? Turn to page 134.

"Let's go, Cornelius! Follow me!"

You dive into the glistening water, the cold pricking your skin like tiny silver knives.

Swimming underwater until your lungs threaten to burst, you surface halfway across the pond. To your surprise, the beasts have stopped at the top of the dune. They move their heads from side to side, searching for you.

Once more you dive out of sight and swim to the far side of the lake. When you surface again, the quagbeasts still seem confused, as if they don't even see you. Finally the leader lets out a thunderous bellow, and the beasts, hanging their monstrous heads, lumber off over the frozen fields.

"Cornelius, they've retreated!" you shout, pulling yourself out of the water onto a snowbank. "And something's very strange," you say. "I'm perfectly dry."

"That's not all that's strange," says the reindeer. "Look, Omina! You have a blue halo around you, like some sort of fog."

"You have one, too!" you say. "And I bet I know what it is—a halo of invisibility! That's why the quagbeasts couldn't see us!"

"The water must be magic! What luck!" cries Cornelius. "And we didn't even have to use your golden whistle!"

"Wait a minute, Cornelius," you say, searching your pockets. "It's gone. The whistle's gone! Maybe I'd better dive back into the water and look for it."

"We don't have time," says the reindeer. "We need to get to Krion's Castle before something happens to Alcazar."

"You're right," you say, hopping onto the reindeer's back. "Who knows how long we'll stay invisible?"

Please turn to page 54.

"As long as we have a peaceful alternative, we should try it," you say. "I know Alcazar would prefer it "

"Excellent decision!" cries ThorTak. "Your stepfather would be proud!" He calls for his hummingbird, who flits over and lights on his hand.

"Gather my Etaks," he commands, and in a flash, he is surrounded by a hundred little brown halflings.

"We are about to save Alcazar and rid the world of that evil wizard, Warzen," he tells them.

The Etaks hug each other in delight and jump up and down.

"I will need mercury," he says to the pink pear Etak, and the halfling scurries off to fetch it.

"I will need gum arabic," he tells the columbine Etak, and off it scampers through the trees.

"Now," says ThorTak when the Etaks return, "I will need you all to be very quiet when Warzen walks out onto his rooftop."

You all stand and watch the far rooftop expectantly.

The moment the wizard appears on his cas tle roof, the Etaks are silent, and ThorTak closes his eyes and extends both hands toward Warzen. You can feel the energy building and building in his great body, and suddenly you seem very, very small next to this huge, powerful presence.

You watch breathlessly when, right before your eyes, a big puff of blue smoke streaks from ThorTak's hands, shoots across the sky, and surrounds the Winter Wizard. Before Warzen can defend himself—POOF! He disappears, and in his place, sprouting right from the rooftop, is a delicate yellow flower.

"You've turned him into a daffodil!" you cry.

"Now he's just like all the flowers he destroyed with his spell," says ThorTak.

The Etaks are jumping up and down, all excited.

"Here, take this cup of nectar to Alcazar," ThorTak tells his Etaks. He hands them a golden chalice filled with clear red liquid. "Go by way of the underground tunnel to the mainland. Have him drink the entire potion, and he will be cured."

"I want to go with them!" you cry.

"No, no. They will bring Alcazar back here in a matter of moments," says ThorTak. "Now be off with you."

The Etaks dance down the petal path, laughing and singing with joy.

"And now we will have a daffodil planting ritual," says ThorTak. With the flick of a finger, he brings the daffodil from the castle rooftop right into your hand.

"I'd say the wizard looks better as a flower, wouldn't you?" says ThorTak, laughing. "We're going to plant him right at the corner of the clearing so I can keep an eye on him. If he gives us any trouble, we'll just have to turn him into a rock."

You dig a hole in the ground and plant Warzen right next to a silver apple tree. Just as you finish, who should walk into the clearing but . . .

"Alcazar!" you cry, rushing to hug the wizard. "I'm so happy to see you!"

"You are a brave child, Omina," says your stepfather. "And I see Warzen got the punishment he deserved."

"Omina's choice," says ThorTak. "She decided to fight violence with gentleness, and you should be proud of her. She is always welcome here on the peaceful island of Etaknon."

ThorTak turns to his Etaks. "Well, what are you waiting for? Make the fire, mash the fruit, string the flowers overhead! It's time for a celebration! We shall have a festival around the fire, and Alcazar and Omina will be our guests of honor!"

And as the stars pop one by one into the sky, you feast on the strange and wonderful foods of Etaknon and watch spring return to your kingdom across the sea.

THE END

"All right," you say, still backing away from the lantern. "You can come along with me to destroy Warzen."

Your eyes open wider and wider as you watch a filmy figure appear slowly and clearly before you. An orc, mean and ugly and as white as frost, is indeed attached to the lantern. His body is scarred, and he drags iron chains from his wrists. Your heart begins to freeze with terror.

You feel yourself breaking out in a cold sweat. Your hands are suddenly wrinkled and old—and over your shoulder hangs a lock of your hair, turned gray.

"What are you doing to me?" you cry.

"It seems you are afraid of my tortured body," laughs the ghost. "Didn't you know you would age at the sight of me?"

"No!" you scream, choking with fright. Your iron poker and golden whistle drop from your grip, and you flee in panic, racing across the rocks, turning to the north and then to the south, not knowing where to go.

Everywhere you run, the ghost is right behind, dragging his chains across the rocks.

"Help me!" you cry. "Somebody help me!" But the only answers are echoes from the cliffs and the sound of chains clanking and scraping over the rocks behind you. You run and scream and hope that someone will hear you—hope that this is not . . .

THE END

"Do you promise me I'll be powerful enough to save Alcazar if I eat this ugly thing?" you ask, turning up your nose at the lumpy mushroom.

"I speak nothing but the truth, child," Madame Wortroot answers, a bit of a croak interrupting her smooth, silken voice. "Now, here, you've no time to waste. On to the glories of power!"

With that, she jams the mushroom into your mouth. Closing your eyes tightly, you chew quickly, and your mouth is filled with a bitter, moldy taste.

Suddenly the wind is whirling past you like a hurricane, and you realize you are spinning, spinning out of control, spinning like a toy top. Madame Wortroot's cackling laughter rings in your ears as you twirl wildly, the forest racing past you in a blur of green and gold. Then you screech to a stop and collapse to the ground from dizziness.

The beautiful woman is gone and there stands the bent old hag, laughing, showing her little toadstool teeth.

"Now, cream puff, we shall call you Wortblossom, and you shall wander the forest forever, giving mushrooms to unhappy travelers! Ha!"

"No! You can't do this!" you shout, but your voice is not your own. It creaks and croaks like the witch's. And now you look down to see that your white tunic has changed to black linen. "You can't do this to me!"

You reach for your poker. It is gone, replaced by a burlap sack stuffed with mushrooms. You snatch it up in your wrinkled hands and swing it at Madame Wortroot.

"You'll pay for this, you cruel old hag!"

The clearing echoes with the witch's cackling, and suddenly, in spite of yourself, you are cackling, too. Loud, creaky laughter bursts from your mouth, and you sling your mushrooms over your crooked back and cry, "Mushrooms, anyone? I hold the key to riches and beauty and power, great power. . . ."

THE END

"Go ahead," you tell the Druid. "I'll follow right behind you." Then you turn to the little moth.

"I promised to send you back to Professor Quince, and I always keep my promises," you say, not looking at Luna.

"But night is falling, and you'll never find your way in the darkness of the forest. These woods are not meant for humans, Omina. They're treacherous."

"Go, Luna. I must stick by my word."

Luna flits over to kiss your cheek, and you watch as her little torch flickers on and off and soon disappears into the blackness of the forest.

You spin around to follow the Druid priest back to his grove, and you see that he is gone. He travels quickly.

"I should have asked him to wait," you say, your heart pounding. You speed down the path you came, winding past endless trees, looking for familiar signs to help you find your way. You don't see bramble bushes or buttercups or any of the flowers you recall from the Druid's path, and slowly you realize what you already knew—you are lost.

You scramble up a tree to look for the Druids' fire, but even from a good height, you see nothing but trees. Darkness creeps into the woods, night is falling, and you have no guide to help you. Could this be . . .

THE END?

"Enter through this opening," instructs the Druid priest, and soon you and Luna are deep inside the trunk of the biggest chinaberry tree in the forest. It is very dark and full of damp wood and moss smells.

The Druid priest raises his musical staff and begins to chant some strange mumblings. Just as you feel you are settling in, Luna's wings start to flutter excitedly.

"Wait, Omina!" she cries suddenly, darting from the tree. "You dropped the mushroom! It's lying there on the ground!"

You try to duck out of the tree trunk to snatch up the Crimson Flame, but you hear the Druid say, "It is too late. The spell is cast."

And instantly, there is a flash of bright light all around you, and your head spins with dizziness. Somewhere in the distance Luna's little voice is calling, "Wait for me, Omina! I'm coming with you!"

But you are in another world now, wrapped in pale yellow light and flying through space and time, all alone.

Please turn to page 28.

"Okay, just clear that snow off *Goldie*'s deck and toss me aboard, mate."

You brush off the snow, put the clam and the iron poker into the boat, and shove the boat into the water.

"Beautiful day for sailing, even if it is a trifle nippy," says the clam. "Now raise the sail and get under way. And watch that wind. She's blowing, all right!"

You hoist the sail, and the boat screeches off, nearly throwing you and the clam overboard.

"The other way!" yells the clam. "Pull that sail to the other side!"

"But how?" you shout. "How?"

"The rope, mate. Pull the rope that's attached to the sail!" he snaps. "Oh, my poor *Goldie*. You ARE a landlubber, now, aren't you, mate?"

With the clam hollering at you all the way, you are soon steaming into the little bay of an island lush and green and untouched by Warzen's spell. There is a group of halflings gathered on the shore, waving their arms excitedly and shouting in friendly voices.

"The Etaks, no doubt," you say, running the boat up onto the sand.

"Citizens, I'd like you to meet— What is your name, anyway?" asks the clam as you lift him from the boat onto the shore.

"Omina—" you begin, but the little Etaks cut you off with their bubbly cries.

"Omina! You're Omina, and we're so glad

you've come to visit!" Their brown fingers are touching your hair and your tunic, and they're bestowing on you lavish gifts of fruit and flowers. One gives you an armful of columbines, and another hands you orchids. There are Etaks with pink pears, and Etaks with tiny purple birds, and Etaks carrying baskets of passionflowers.

You are soon buried in presents, from chin to toe, and you don't quite know what to do.

Please turn to page 63.

"Here," you say, handing the professor the golden whistle. "Take this."

He rubs it delicately between his thumb and forefinger, examining it as if it were a specimen.

"Where did you get this? This is a wizard's tool, not a child's toy."

"Exactly," you answer. "It belongs to my stepfather, the Wizard Alcazar. But it is merely a deposit for your luna, and I expect you to return it when I bring her back."

"Don't worry. I have no time for toys or magic or silly wizardry," he grumbles. He drops the whistle into a desk drawer and goes back to his work on the peacock butterfly—fastening its wings with thin strips of paper. "Now be off, the two of you. I have an important job to complete here."

The moth flutters to your shoulder and whispers in your ear. "You can call me Luna. What's your name?"

"I'm Omina."

"Okay, Omina, let's go."

You head out into the trees, the luna darting to and fro before you, her antenna glowing like a tiny torch in the darkness of the tree shadows.

"I bet you're glad to be away from him aren't you, Luna?"

"You mean Professor Quince? Oh, I don't know. He's been good to me. He keeps me even though I'm ugly, with my antenna missing and all. . . ."

"Luna," you say, "I don't think you're ugly at all. In fact," you add quietly, "I think you're beautiful."

The moth blushes peach and shakes her head. "No, no. I'm not even good enough to be one of Professor Quince's specimens."

"Who cares? Having two antennae is very common—and look where it got all those other butterflies."

"You're just trying to cheer me up," says Luna, her voice quivering a bit.

"Not at all, Luna. I really think you're very special."

"Strange, you mean."

You stop short.

"Come here and sit on the back of my hand," you tell the moth firmly, in a tone you learned from Alcazar. "Now, listen to me. It's Erasmus Quince who's strange, not you. Think of all the things you can do that those other moths never dreamed of. You can talk, you can light up the darkness, you can even make somebody a fine friend. The rest of them have to settle for just being pretty."

Luna's blush is now a deep orange, and she flutters her wing bashfully in front of her eyes. You sigh in frustration.

"Come on now, Luna. Let's get on our way."

As you set off down the path again, you realize you are right in the middle of a pine woods so thick with snowy branches that you can't even get through. The treetops are black with crows.

"Oh, no!" you moan. "What do we do now? Go back the other way?"

"We can't. This is the safest path to the Druids," says Luna. "I can fly in and out between the branches, but I'll have to be careful of those crows. But I don't know how you're going to get through, Omina."

"It looks as if I'll just have to chop my way through with my poker. Here, shine your light over on this branch, will you, Luna?"

You grasp your poker in both hands and hack a snow-covered branch off the nearest fir tree. Out of nowhere comes a tortured bellow, like the cry of a great animal in agony.

"What is that?" you whisper, your eyes searching the forest for some hidden hairy beast.

"I can't tell," says Luna. "Let's keep going."

Slash! Off comes another branch, followed by a low, pain-filled moan.

Luna's wings are fluttering excitedly now, like a bee's. "Oh, my gosh, Omina, look! I think you hurt that poor tree!" She shines her light on the trunk where the limb broke off, and there you see drops of blood oozing from the wound.

"I had no idea—" you cry, but Luna cuts you off.

"Omina! The trees are moving in on us. We've got to get out of here!"

All around you, big, snowy trees are creep ing closer, their branches outstretched and full of crows. You hold your poker across your

chest and watch as they move closer, closer, making the forest floor tremble as if in an earthquake.

"Omina! What are we going to do?"

You must make a decision quickly, and you have two choices:

1) Talk to the trees and hope they will understand. Turn to page 59.

2) Run back the way you came. Turn to page 50.

You wave good-bye to the tiny army and go back inside the castle to sit on a snow mound. It's very lonely, and you can't stop wondering whether or not you made the right decision.

Days and nights pass when every minute you think you hear Fiffergrund's voice outside, or see Alcazar walking through the doorway. You are cold and hungry and can barely sleep more than an hour at a time.

Soon a week has passed, and there is still no sign of your companions. One morning, you wrap your cloak around you and, weak and miserable, start off toward home.

Did your friends ever get to Warzen's Castle, or were they captured by the orcs on the way? Perhaps they gave up, leaving Alcazar to die in the Ice Cavern.

If you had found the courage to help them in battle, maybe Warzen would have been conquered by now and you and Alcazar would be on your way home together.

But you will never know. Because this is . . .

THE END

"I think it's best for me just to be on my way. Warzen's Castle isn't all that far from here," you say. "And I'm really a terrible sailor."

"Suit yourself," snaps the clam. "But don't come crawling back for help later. I gave you your chance."

You wrap your cloak tightly around you and head off over the icy rocks toward the north. As you trudge along, the snow begins to fall, and soon you are in the middle of a storm that whips ice and sleet into your face. Your hands and feet are growing numb, and you hurry onward to reach the castle before it gets worse. Suddenly a thought occurs to you.

"Once I get to Warzen's Castle, I'll need help to get by the orcs and boars," you think. "And I'll never find help in the middle of a blizzard! Perhaps I'd better go back and try to make it to Etaknon after all."

You turn back, the wind now pounding you from behind. But before you go far at all, you hear the sound of a voice shouting from the cliffs above.

"There's that child of Alcazar's! Let's get her!"

You look and see twenty orc boarkeepers charging over the rocks toward you, their rusty swords and pigstickers flying in all directions. They are snorting, and their boars are snorting, and you run as fast as you can.

"Get me back to the clam," you tell your feet, trying to make them go more quickly.

But you are not fast enough. The orcs are

soon upon you, tying you up and taking you away on a big, ugly boar.

"Well, you'll get to see your wizard after all," sneers one.

"Yeah, you'll have plenty of time to catch up on the news while you hang next to him in the Ice Cavern!" howls another.

You are silent. You realize that you are powerless and that now it is too late to do anything, anyway. Alcazar's words ring in your head: "They are an army, and you are but one."

THE END

"We're all in this together," you say, joining the others outside, "and I'm coming, too."

Fiffergrund slips his arm through yours, shouting, "We'll fight to the end."

"Onward!" calls Krion. You all follow him around the back to the frost-covered stables. "Now, watch this!"

With one snap of the giant's fingers, hundreds of silver pegasi soar into the air, flapping crystalline wings as delicate as dragonflies', their feathery manes shimmering in the cold.

"What's that?" you ask as an enormous white dragon, its teeth bared, flies out of the stables.

"My leader pegasus turned into a dragon?" roars Krion. "Oh, I'll get back at you for this, Warzen, believe me!" he cries, shaking his scepter at the sky.

He lifts you and Fiffergrund onto your pegasus and turns toward Cornelius.

"Now, what shall we do with you, reindeer? Let me see. . . ." He plucks a feather from a wing of a pegasus and strokes it across Cornelius's back.

"There, now you shall fly like a bird," says Krion, and, magically, the reindeer floats right off the ground.

Krion mounts the gigantic white dragon, and off you all fly, into the crisp, clean air.

Soon jagged cliffs loom high above the seacoast. Atop them stands a monstrous stone structure, turned black with age and crawling

with boars. At the sight of the winged army, the pigs start charging excitedly from one end of the moat to the other, snorting high-pitched warning signals to their masters. A few boars fall headlong into the moat, splashing and squealing.

Krion raises his ice scepter and shouts to the pegasi, "Let them sleep!"

With that, the steeds shake their manes and a cloud of dust sparkles down onto the boars like new snow. They soon stumble and topple on one another, falling deeply asleep and snoring loudly.

"Good work!" shouts the giant. "They won't wake up for hours!"

You follow Krion's dragon as it swoops over the piles of sleeping boars and lands next to the entrance of the castle. On Krion's command, the huge door creaks open, so you jump off your steeds and make your way into the damp darkness of Warzen's halls. Far down the passageway, you hear singing and shouting, as if the boarkeepers are partying.

"Good timing," you think to yourself. "They're playing instead of guarding the castle!"

"This way," whispers the wizard as he creeps down a stairwell to the right of the doorway. The four of you descend the spiral steps and tiptoe into a musty tunnel, weapons drawn. Water drips from the moat above, and the cold creeps up your spine and into your very bones.

"Look! The Ice Cavern!" cries Cornelius—too loudly—as he dashes toward a rusty iron door at the far end of the tunnel. You are instantly at his side, smashing at the lock with your poker, when the scrambling of feet echoes from behind. In a moment, the boarkeepers are rushing at you savagely, their torches and pigstickers flying in all directions.

Suddenly, a voice booms down the corridor. "Halt, boarkeepers!"

There, at the entrance to the tunnel, stands Warzen, his jagged teeth shining in the torchlight.

"Leave these brave creatures to me," he says, his icy beard nearly cracking from his evil grin. "I will personally see to it that they enjoy the last few moments of their puny lives. Now, let's see . . . . Shall I handle them one at a time, or shall I just destroy all four with one blow?"

He taps his staff in his palm, thinking. "One by one would be fun, now, wouldn't it? Ah, yes. Let's start with you, frost giant. I think you'd make a very fine ice statue, very fine."

Krion shoots a quick glance at Fiffergrund, as if asking a question.

"Just stay right there," whispers the elf. "I'll handle it."

"You'll handle it, you hairy little elf?" sneers Warzen, laughing. "Wait your turn. You'll have plenty of work trying to fend for yourself when the time comes."

He raises his staff, and—POOF!—a bolt of icy blue lightning shoots toward Krion. In a split second, Fiffergrund bolts in front of the giant, holding the topaz between his fingers. The lightning strikes the jewel, bounces off, and streaks back at Warzen, striking him between the eyes. Before he can even cry out, the Winter Wizard lights up like a blue comet, glowing in the darkness of the tunnel. A moment later, he stands frozen a huge chunk of ice.

Terrified, the boarkeepers run away helter-skelter through the tunnel and trample each other in their rush to get up the staircase.

"You did it, Fiffergrund!" you shout with joy. "That was spectacular, wasn't it, Cornelius?" As you turn toward the reindeer, he purrs contentedly. "Cornelius, you're a cat again!"

"And I'm a wizard again," says Krion, "and happy to shed my giant body!" He turns toward the Ice Cavern door. "Now for our real mission," he says, and pointing a finger shatters the heavy lock.

You rush into the cavern, but it is pitch dark, and you squint to adjust your eyes. Right in front of you is a huge boar, hanging upside down by its hooves. Its mouth has dropped open, and its glassy eyes stare into eternity. "It's dead," you murmur, and you turn away.

You squint again and discover that there, next to the boar, hangs Alcazar. His wrists are

torn and bleeding from the rusty chains. The bottom of his nightshirt is ripped to shreds. His face is drawn, pale, and scratched, but . . . you gasp with joy . . . unlike the boar, he is alive!

"Alcazar!" you cry as you throw your arms around his frail body. "I'm so glad you are all right."

In a moment, Krion is at your side, and at a flick of his hand, Alcazar's chains part and drop to the ground.

"You are a brave soldier, Omina," says Alcazar. "A very brave soldier. I am proud of what you have done."

"Now it's time this wizard was well again," pipes Fiffergrund, hopping to Alcazar's side. "Krion, could you please transport a Crimson Flame Mushroom from the forest to us here?"

"I'm sure I can," he answers, closing his eyes. Within moments, a bright red mushroom is in his hand. "For you, Alcazar," he says, "and may you and the kingdom never fall ill again."

With just one bite of the mushroom, the twinkle is back in Alcazar's eye. The color rushes into his cheeks. "Let's get out of here!" he says energetically the minute he is back on his feet.

Outside, you mount your steeds and take off into the star-studded sky. A gust of warm, southerly wind blows through your hair and takes you by surprise.

"Spring, Cornelius! Spring, Alcazar!" you

cry. "Spring is returning to the kingdom! Winter is over!"

Tiny green and yellow shoots are pushing through the ground below, and you know that by the time the snow has thawed, you and Alcazar and Cornelius will be back to stirring a fine potful of soup over your very own fire.

THE END

Poker in hand, you back away from the lantern, then race as fast as you can over the rocks toward the north. Water, frigid and foamy, splashes up into your boots, but you keep running, not once looking back.

The wind stings your face, and your lungs burn from cold air, but you run on, with only thoughts of Alcazar's fevered face to keep you from collapsing. At last the wailing of the ghost ceases, and you can see no trace of the lantern behind you.

"Whew! That was a close one," you say, collapsing on a big flat rock. "And night is falling already . . . ."

Wrapping your cloak about you, you lie down to rest for a few moments. Your eyelids are heavy, and before you know it, you float off into a deep sleep.

Suddenly you are jolted awake by an eerie rumbling deep beneath the rocks. You sit straight up, your hand reaching for the iron poker. The rumbling grows louder, louder, until, moved by the thunderous power of an earthquake, the boulders around you begin to shake and roll.

Huge crevices open between the rocks, and heavy snow slides down into the openings. You clutch your cloak to your heart and stare in horror as hundreds of flowers rise out of the cracks, right through the snow.

"Oh, it's only lilies," you say and sigh with relief. But then you see they are still growing. They are not the peaceful Easter lilies of

spring, but heavy, monstrous flowers as white and cold as the moon, soaring as high as oak trees. They are bending their petals in your direction as though they have eyes, as though they can see you.

A strange sound begins to roll from their thick throats. They are growling at you like animals, lowering their heads until you can see the insides of their petals. They have long, rubbery tongues, and mouths that open and close as if searching hungrily for prey.

"Man-eaters!" you whisper, your mouth dry with fear. The growling grows louder, and now the thick green tongues are just inches from your face. You must think quickly, before the monster lilies turn on you.

You have three choices:

1) If you feel brave enough to attack the lilies, turn to page 58.

2) If you prefer to use magic and blow your golden whistle, turn to page 13.

3) If you just want to hide under your cloak until dawn and hope they disappear with the sunrise, turn to page 20.

"Quick, Luna, hide in my pocket," you whisper. She wriggles into your tunic, and you work your way beneath a pile of snow-covered branches. Reaching out, you pull more branches over your body and lie motionless on your back.

"Be as quiet as possible," you tell Luna.

The snorts and yelps of the army are muffled now, and the battle seems to be dying down. You wonder who is winning, the trees or the orcs.

"Let's get out of here before the trees hurt anyone else!" shouts an orc.

You hear feet scrambling and squeaking over the snowy ground, and a few boars grunt wearily. Suddenly a gruff voice cries, "The child! Where's the blasted child?"

The army is up for grabs again.

"It's all your fault, Gorff, you stupid pig head!" shouts an orc.

"Oh, yeah? I was fighting to protect your hog head, Krogg! I should have let those trees knock you out cold!"

"Why, you bloody nitwit!". comes the reply. "I'll teach you a lesson, I will!" Your hear orc swords smashing against each other.

Another voice yells, "I'm not gonna stay here and get my hide whipped. Come on, Thaug. Just leave them to their bickering."

"Wait for me!" hollers Gorff.

Soon the squabbling noises fade off in the distance, and you peek through the branches to see if the coast is clear. There are orcs lying motionless on the forest floor, and torn branches scattered everywhere. The trees are moaning very quietly, blood oozing down their trunks.

"I think both sides lost," you whisper to Luna, "and they don't have the energy left to come after us. Just stay in my pocket and tell me how to get to the Druids from here."

"It sounded as if the orcs went south, the wrong way," says Luna. "So just take the path to the right and we should be safe."

You creep quietly past the wound trees, stepping over orc bodies, and soon you are heading along a well-traveled path to the north.

Please turn to page 74

You grab a handful of icicles from an ice cliff and dive for shelter behind the dune.

"Cornelius! Come quickly!" you cry, and in a flash, the reindeer is beside you.

"I'm going to try to frighten them off," you tell him as you hurl icicles at the quagbeasts. Cornelius shakes his head in frustration as he watches them bounce off the approaching animals harmlessly.

"Omina, they can't even feel them," moans the reindeer. "The beasts aren't even blinking, and they're making headway fast. We've got to do something to stop them! What else can we use against them?"

"What about snowballs, Cornelius? The snow is heavy and should pack well." You scoop up a handful and form it into a hard, icy ball. You hurl it, and it hits one of the beasts right between the eyes.

"It's useless!" cries Cornelius as the animals continue to stampede toward you. The leader of the pack is so close now that you can see the foam dripping from its jagged teeth. Its eye is clotted shut with blood from its wound.

Suddenly it lets out an enraged howl and charges toward you, its hooves digging into the ice. You back down the dune to the water's edge and turn to see that the beast is at the very top of the hill, ready to attack.

"He'll rip us to shreds in no time!" shouts Cornelius. "It's hopeless."

You think quickly. The pool is right behind

you, and the golden whistle is snug in your pocket.

"No, Cornelius. There is still hope," you say, trying to sound confident.

You have a split second to make another choice.

Please go back to page 46
and make another choice

"Well I'll just stay for the night," you tell the Etaks, who jump up and down excitedly. "But I'll have to leave in the morning, after I make a plan to rescue Alcazar."

"You can make your plans in due time" says one Etak, pulling you outside to a chair in the sun. "Now sit down and make yourself comfortable. We will bring you some lunch."

"I'd like to see if you can help me with Warzen, too. . . ."

"Don't worry. Everything in its time," says another Etak.

Soon little Etaks are feeding your strange foods that taste surprisingly wonderful. There are yellow fruits, mashed up and served on long green leaves. There are rich pink nectars to drink from coconut shells. And for dessert, they serve you purple flower petals.

"Glazed with moonflower honey," they tell you. Slowly, slowly you feel very content to sit in the sun and rest, not wanting to rush back to the cold and snowy mainland. The afternoon passes softly, and soon it is evening, and then morning again, and you are happy to sit in the sunlight, eating sweet and colorful concoctions.

As the days go by, you forget completely about Warzen and winter and all the terrible events that brought you to this island, and you live long and happy days relaxing with the little brown Etaks in their paradise.

THE END

You and Luna follow the Druid back again along the winding forest paths, past bramble bushes, and into the clearing where the robed figures are warming themselves by the fire. The Druid priest taps his staff on an enormous tree and out comes a white unicorn, as beautiful as a picture in a book.

"I've never seen a real unicorn before," you tell Luna. "It's gorgeous."

"Think of your destination and you will be there in the wink of an eye," says the Druid. "Go in peace."

You call, "Thank you," just as the unicorn soars off.

In a blink, Warzen's castle is before you, tall and black and crawling with boars.

"I was here once as a child, with Alcazar," you say. "I seem to remember an outside entrance to the Ice Cavern back by the hill. Let's see if we can find it."

The unicorn follows your directions and comes to a halt just on the other side of the rocky knoll. You dismount and creep to the top of the hill. There, just a stone's throw away, you can see a lone orc guarding an entrance to a cave.

"The Ice Cavern is underground," you say. "And I think it's connected to the castle by a tunnel. Let's wait for the changing of the guard and sneak in when their backs are turned."

When you look around, the unicorn has disappeared, as quietly as a breeze. As darkness falls, the orc goes off duty and the new guard stops to talk to him. Their backs are turned to you.

"Quick, let's go!" says Luna, and you dart through the door. Inside, hanging from chains on the icy stone walls, are orcs and boars. They are nearly lifeless, their bodies raw from beating, with gray patches of frostbite on their skin. Far in the corner, you see one human, a feeble old man with a long white beard, his wrists torn and bleeding from the rusty chains.

"Alcazar! We're here!" you cry. "We found you, Alcazar!" And you rush to his side to hug him tight. "We have the Crimson Flame, we just came from the Druids on a unicorn, I have a wonderful green moth for a guide, and. . . ." The words spill wildly from your mouth, you are so happy to see him alive.

You give the wizard a few bites of the mushroom, and instantly the color rushes back into his face and he straightens up, smiling. He looks healthy again.

"Omina, you are a brave one," he says, breaking his chains from the wall with little effort. "Now, we have no time to waste. We must capture. Warzen before he knows I'm freed. Come with me into the castle. I have a plan."

You and Luna follow Alcazar as he heads out of an underground tunnel, speeds through a maze of paths, and peeks around a corner where there is a door guarded by an orc.

"The Treasure Room," whispers the wizard, and your heart quickens.

The sound of Alcazar's voice brings the boarkeeper to attention. He raises his pigsticker and is ready to lunge at you when Alcazar points a finger at him, commanding, "Stun!" The guard wavers and collapses, and you step over him as you follow Alcazar into the room.

Your eyes widen in wonder. Big gold nuggets fill the corners, diamonds and emeralds and rubies overflow from leather bags, silver coins and golden chains and precious rings litter the stone floor.

Alcazar spins around, and with a flick of his hand, locks the door behind you. Not wasting a moment, he places an enormous white gem in the center of the room and goes into deep meditation.

"I've seen him like this before, Luna," you tell your friend quietly. "This is a most important spell. We must allow him peace and quiet so he can concentrate fully."

Luna nods her head and waits silently.

You jump as the Treasure Room door suddenly splinters into a thousand pieces, wooden chips flying about the room, and Warzen storms in, his voice bellowing.

"Intruders!" He points his staff at you, ready to attack. "For this you shall die!" His eyes are black fire, and his teeth are glinting like a wild boar's, ready and eager to tear your flesh to bits.

You turn to Alcazar, panic in your eyes, and see that he is ignoring the wicked wizard, still deep in concentration on the jewel.

Warzen raises his staff over Alcazar, shouting, "You fool of a wizard! I shall turn you—"

Before he can finish, there is a great burst of light in the room, shooting through the gem, bright as the light of the sun. The light pulsates everywhere, white and hot, blinding you, forcing Luna down beneath your cloak, trembling.

Then, as suddenly as it appeared, the light disappears, and all is dark again. You open your eyes and look around.

"Warzen!" you shout. "Warzen's gone!"

"He is gone from this world, my child," says Alcazar, staring calmly into the gem, which is now as black as coal. "I've entrapped him, body and soul, in the jewel. He will never be a problem for us again."

Your heart soars, and you step out into the daylight to see the boars and orcs scattering in all directions.

"They are lost without their leader," says Alcazar.

"Look!" shouts Luna. "The snow is melting! And little green shoots are coming through the ground."

"Oh, Alcazar, spring is returning to the kingdom!'

"Come, Omina. Come, Luna. It is time we are leaving. We are going home."

Luna's golden eyes widen. "You mean I

don't have to go back to Professor Quince?"

"That's entirely up to you," says Alcazar, stroking the moth's fuzzy head. "If you have learned just one lesson from this journey, it should be that you are special and worth a great deal to yourself and to all of us. Without your courage and guidance, we might not have made it."

A little tear, golden and delicate, drops from Luna's eye. "And Professor Quince doesn't own me, does he? I am free to make my own decision?"

Alcazar nods.

"Then I'm going with you and Omina. I'm going home."

You hook your hand in Alcazar's belt, and with Luna flitting to and fro before you, you head off over the crocus fields toward home.

THE END

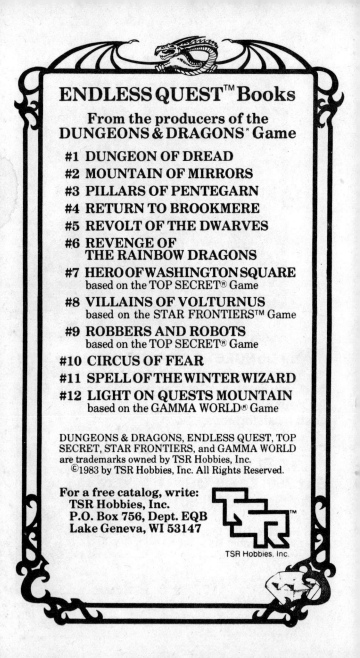

ENDLESS QUEST™ Books

From the producers of the DUNGEONS & DRAGONS™ Game

For a free catalog, write:
TSR Hobbies, Inc.
P.O. Box 756, Dept. EQB
Lake Geneva, WI 53147

TSR Hobbies, Inc.